Berto's World

Berto's World

STORIES

R. A. Comunale, M.D.

MOUNTAIN LAKE PRESS

MOUNTAIN LAKE PARK, MARYLAND

ALSO BY R.A. COMUNALE

Requiem for the Bone Man
The Legend of Safehaven

LIBRARY OF CONGRESS
CONTROL NUMBER: 2008908390

ISBN: 978-0-9814773-2-9

ISBN-10: 0-9814773-2-1

COPYRIGHT © 2008 R.A. COMUNALE

ALL RIGHTS RESERVED

PRINTED IN THE UNITED STATES OF AMERICA

MOUNTAIN LAKE PRESS
24 D STREET
MOUNTAIN LAKE PARK, MD 21550

FIRST EDITION, OCTOBER 2008

BOOK AND COVER DESIGN BY MICHAEL HENTGES

CONTENTS

To the Dr. Agnellis of the world

I am now more than three-score-and-ten years old—but once I was a boy.

My name is Robert Anthony Galen, M.D., retired.

I was born Roberto Antonio Galen. Save for the whimsical stroke of an immigration official's pen on Ellis Island, it would have been Gallini, my father's given name in the old country.

I live now with my friends at the Pennsylvania mountaintop retreat called Safehaven. The three of us—Bob Edison, his wife Nancy, and I—await the winding down of our lives on a mountain blessed with the magic of love and the vagaries of memory. We feel the sere chill of the one visitor we cannot turn away. The Bone Man will come to each of us at his whim and in due time.

But for now I sit in my room and stare out the window overlooking the mountain vista, and I remember. I remember the boy I once was and the people I loved. In that distant past I roamed my world as a child—a child named Berto.

I am an old man now. I easily fall asleep at my little desk and I dream. I dream of being that young boy once more. I dream of Berto's world.

The Flower

I was eight years old when I had my first date.

No, I wasn't strange or precocious, at least not that way.

But she was dead.

It was one of those Indian-summer late-September Saturdays: no school, breezes warm yet crisp, with the feel of impending seasonal change lurking behind each gust. Angie and I—my best friend Angelo—as all normal, eight-year-old boys are wont to do, hung out and tried to stay out of trouble at the same time.

Fat chance.

We often wandered away from our tenement neighborhood. That weekend we were explorers seeking the mysteries beyond our little, multiethnic, low-income ghetto. It really wasn't that far—two blocks past the grammar school run by nuns who dressed like penguins, turn left at the cemetery, then go another six blocks past the central business district. And there we were.

It might as well have been another planet, another universe.

There were houses, big houses. Almost as big as the multifamily buildings we were crowded into in numbers too large to count. But, wonder of wonders, these houses held only one family, and often that family was just two people.

We stared up from our eight-year-old vantages at the brick and wood-sided edifices with their expanses of green grass and shrub-filled lawns, and their semicircular, concrete driveways leading up to side attachments that were larger than the little apartment Mama, Papa, and I lived in. They held no people; they were garages, homes for the automobiles that the teeming masses we belonged to could only dream of obtaining.

It's funny, the bittersweet memories of that walk on the bright side. We were children who would easily have fit into Dickens's London as chimney sweeps: runny noses, uncombed hair, torn corduroy pants our mamas had found at the church's basement thrift shop, worn brown shoes and pullover sweaters that had served former owners until they no longer filled their fashion needs. In another time and place we would have been called ragamuffins.

Even in the early fall weather there were things that attracted us just as they did the bees and colorful birds smart enough to survive there. We saw the multihued heads of summer- and fall-blooming flowers.

The frost would not carry them off for weeks.

It wasn't until I was much older that I learned their names: marigolds, geraniums, impatiens, and pansies. Climbing roses filled out trellises along the front windows. In our own little tenement world, the nearest thing we had were the ever-present weeds and unstoppable dandelions that the old nannas would pluck and turn into ethnic salads—unless the men decided to ferment them. It wasn't just grapes or potato skins that could produce Lethean drinks, imbibed to forget what one did or where one lived.

I was eight years old, and I was bold. I dared tempt the Fates by taking off my shoes and patched socks. I wanted to feel the tingle of grass under my feet.

Angelo laughed as he flipped off his shoes and socks, too

"*Berto, siete pazzesch!*"

You're crazy, Berto!

"In modo da siete voi, Angie!"

So are you, Angie!

Yes, we were both crazy. We ran back and forth across that lawn and the ones next to it, the green blades tickling the bottoms of our feet, our toes taking on the hue of string beans. I bent over and picked a golden marigold. The curiosity that in later life brought me pleasure and grief made me start to chew on it. It was like the spinach Mama would make, a mixture of bitter and sweet.

"Hey, you two, get outta here! You don't belong here! Go back to your own place!"

We stopped in mid-step and turned to see two ladies, one older and one younger, standing at the front door of the big brick house. The girl couldn't have been more than a teenager. She seemed strangely out of proportion with her long, slender legs and arms. Her dress, a walking kaleidoscope of floral print, seemed ill-fitting around her waist. Her head bent forward, and the occasional wisp of wind stirred the long blonde hair about her face.

We were only eight, but even then we could tell she was pretty. I liked her in an innocent, youthful way. She was crying. She looked up at me and our eyes locked, her grass-green irises a counterpoint to her marigold hair.

"I'll call the police if you don't leave!"

The older woman's voice was shrill and penetrating.

I looked at Angie. He shrugged and picked up his shoes and socks, and I did the same. We walked barefoot down the slate sidewalk, our heads half-turned toward that house of flowers, where we saw a man come out and raise the garage door. We stopped and watched as a big black car pulled out, and the two women got into the back seat. It drove off in the opposite direction.

I looked at Angie, and he looked at me. We grinned and ran back to that forbidden lawn and let it tickle our feet and our fancy once more. We sat on it, rolled on it, then lay down and stared at the sky. I can understand why Eve ate the apple.

Strange, even now I can see that cloudless blue sky, a clear blue I have beheld only in the eyes of girls I dated at university. I can also recall the fear in that young girl's green eyes, as she climbed awkwardly into that big black car.

We must have dozed off. Suddenly the growl of an engine brought us back to reality, before the car rolled into view. We jumped up and ran behind one of the large maple trees lining the street. We watched as the great sedan pulled into the driveway and stopped. Only the man and the older woman got out and walked into the house.

Angie and I put our socks and shoes on and trudged back to our own world.

The following weekend was still warm—warm enough for the two of us to go hunting for soda-pop bottles and coins thrown into the nearby river. The deposits on the bottles were our only source of spending money at that stage of life. The coins paid by the local butcher/grocery-store owner were gifts from heaven, responses to our prayers as we knelt in the pews of the Catholic church attached to the grammar school we attended.

We walked down Fulton Street with its eponymous Fulton's Tavern and numerous, decaying, antebellum clapboard houses, places that made our tenements look like luxury apartments. They flanked the banks of the river and, so I was told, it was not unusual for the entire bottom floors of those places to flood. Even now the lesson remains: There is always someone worse off, someone a rung higher on the pain ladder.

The warm weather had brought out the old folks in the neighborhood.

Angie stopped me.

"Berto, look at the Mustache Petes!"

We watched, as the old men pretended to be boys like us, twisting and pirouetting like grotesque ballerinas, as they cast balls playing boccie. We giggled, then laughed out loud, and some of them turned and directed evil eyes at us for being rude and, probably, for being young.

So we walked quickly past the men and headed down the alleyway between the tavern and its neighboring house. I looked at the window of the tavern and saw the incongruous ROOMS TO LET sign. Who lived in a tavern? It was one of those later-teen-year epiphanies when I learned who—and what. But when you are eight, "red-light ladies" and "back-room abortionists" mean nothing.

The riverbank was slightly muddy from the previous night's shower. We slid and stumbled and finally arrived at a spot low enough to walk on the stones sticking up from the shallow water. It was a banner harvest, as we pulled out the casually discarded bottles, mentally adding up the two cents each would bring at the little shop run by the man everyone in the neighborhood called the Mad Russian.

Angie saw it first. I had bent over to pull out a buffalo nickel wedged in-between two river rocks. I was excited. A nickel went a long way then. I got ready to yell out my find, when Angie's cry startled me into silence.

"Berto, look, over there!"

He was shaking and pointing, even forgetting to stand on the flat stone that had kept him relatively dry. I turned to where he was pointing—one of the pylons under the Central River Bridge—and saw it.

At first it seemed to be just a bundle of rags. Not unusual around here, something saved to clean or mend or fix other things with. Who would be so foolish as to discard something useful in the river?

Then I saw the arm sticking out.

I moved toward it, even as I heard Angie running away, the splashes of his panicked flight casting a spray. He reached the bank and scrambled up. From the corner of my eye I saw his wet and muddied pants disappear back into the alleyway.

The bundle lay there, river water covering and uncovering it with silt. As some of the mud washed away, I saw the floral-print dress. I moved closer.

My lady stared at me with sunken, vacant, green eyes. Her blonde tresses, waterlogged, swayed with the river current. Her long arms and slender legs looked like some mishandled rag doll, twisted in ways I did not think possible. The light-pink lipstick failed to conceal the blue-black discoloration of her lips and half-protruding tongue.

She was dead.

In some respects death was no stranger to our neighborhood. There was the dog hit by a car lying in the gutter, its hind legs stiffened and spread. There was the drunk who fell into that final, cheap, alcohol-induced coma and never woke up—lying in his own urine, feces, and vomit. There was the common-law wife choked and thrown out the window of a third-story walk-up, sprawled on the street like a distorted pretzel, while the police led her drunken, half-naked husband away. And, often, there was the young male killed in an ethnic clash down on Hamilton Street.

My lady was different.

She didn't belong in the river. She shouldn't be here, discarded. She shouldn't have died. Someone like her belonged in a place of green and rainbow colors, running barefoot and letting the grass caress her toes.

Damn! I never realized that even as a kid I was a romantic.

I stared at her, taking in the cyans, fuscias, and browns of her hands and feet. I looked once more into those green eyes and thought, "I'm sorry, lady."

Don't leave me!

Yes, I heard it—no, not with my ears, in my mind.

Don't leave me! I want to go home!

I heard myself reply out loud, "Okay, lady."

I turned and walked back to the riverbank, the treasure trove of soda pop bottles Angie and I had collected splayed nearby. I left them. Maybe they would still be there later, maybe not. There were other enterprising kids in the neighborhood.

Papa went to the police station. I saw the wagon and heard the siren, as it headed toward the river. And then I waited.

I told Mama I was going out to play again. She patted my head. I could see she was worried about my experience.

I snuck in by the side door. In those days they took the accidentally and deliberately dead to the police station. The big door at the end of the ground floor beckoned me forward with its mysterious letters: MORGUE.

I opened that heavy oak door, and the odors from within caressed my olfactory nerves for the first time. The mixed perfumes of formaldehyde and decaying flesh became old friends in later years, as I made my way through medical school.

On that day my lady lay there in repose, her floral-print dress and undergarments resting in a box on the floor next to the table that had become her bedroom suite. She was the center of attention to the two men dressed in long, priest-like gowns and dark-brown, elbow-length gloves, their faces masked and their heads skull-capped.

I was eight years old and I was bold.

"Why did she die?"

They looked up, and one yelled for me to get out. The other paused then asked me the question that opened up the door to the rest of my life.

"Why do you want to know, kid?"

I didn't hesitate. The answer was already within me—I just didn't know it until then.

"I want to be like you."

In the few seconds of silence that followed, I walked over to where my lady—my human marigold—lay. I looked at her, eyes now closed, face in sleep-like calm. No, she didn't smile—she couldn't. But my mind heard her once more.

Thank you!

The Mad Russian

They call it the Widow Maker, but I've been a widower twice, so it's a moot point for me.

I lay there on the table in the special-procedures room, while my cardiologist and former student Dr. Salvatore Crescenzi threaded the catheter up from my thigh and into my heart. I watched the screen above my head, blurred by the slight haze of medication, as the catheter tip entered the left coronary artery and Sal injected the dye.

I must have said something out loud, because he stopped and asked if anything was wrong.

Forgive me, dear reader, but I almost giggled—I did giggle.

Damned medication!

"No, I just had three random thoughts run across my geriatric cortex."

"You goin' senile on me, Galen?"

"Hope not. I can still recognize a major blockage in my old friend, the LAD, when I see it. Right?"

"Damn, sure enough, old man. Looks like a ninety-five-percent stenosis of the left anterior descending coronary artery. Okay, hang on. You know what I gotta do."

I sure did. Even with the pain and twilight-sedation drugs in me, I felt myself tightening up a bit. A little knowledge is a dangerous thing. I knew he had to do balloon angioplasty, using an expanding, balloon-tipped catheter to break through the blockage, and then install a stent to keep the artery open.

Not bad for an almost-octogenarian retired doctor, eh?

"Do you feel anything, Galen?"

"Boy, if I had you back in my classroom you'd feel something about now. 'Course I feel something! Get on with it."

Soon he did, and I saw the dye course through the stent-widened, left anterior descending artery in my heart, carrying its river of life to my poor old myocardium.

"Ain't science wonderful, Crescenzi?"

"Yep! Now what were those other two thoughts crossing your non-existent neurons?"

I giggled again. The SOB must have given me more pain meds through my IV.

"Well," and then I knew for sure, as my speech slurred slightly, "now I can attend the wedding of you and your lover."

Crescenzi was the best damned interventional cardiologist around. He also was gay. Back when he was my student it was all I could do to keep some Luddite profs from having him expelled for "unspecified reasons."

"And the other?"

As I drifted off I mumbled, "My first real haircut."

When you live hand-to-mouth, some of the niceties of the middle class are a luxury. Include haircuts in that category.

Papa and Mama would take turns putting a bowl over my head when my hair got too shaggy for them to tolerate, as well as the nuns at my grammar school. I didn't feel bad. All my friends got the same kind of haircut and, sometimes, those without a mama—like Salvatore—would come over, and my folks would do the honors.

Recipe: Take one pot or, more commonly, one soup bowl, and place over squirming kid's head.

Then take pair of scissors, better known as shears.

Cut whatever hair sticks out from under the mold.

Complete the process and *voila!* You get a very bad but functional, marine-style haircut—at no cost, except the other kids making fun of you. But usually they didn't. We all looked the same, and the nuns just ignored it as a fact of life in our neighborhood.

I had just turned seven that early spring day, and Papa was enjoying one of his rare days off. He must have been feeling exceptionally good. After I had blown out the candles on the three cupcakes—our substitute for a cake—he stood up, looked at me and Mama, and said, "Berto, we go for a walk."

I guess it was his old-country way of father-son bonding. It didn't matter to me. I was ecstatic. I would get to spend more time with Papa!

It was still chilly, so we put on our church-basement-sale jackets then headed down the stairs and out. We didn't wear hats or gloves. We were men.

I remember running to catch up with him, as he strode down the street. He wasn't a tall man, but he could move like one, and I had to shout at him to slow down. He turned and saw me puffing to catch up, and he actually laughed out loud.

Papa almost never laughed.

We walked across the river bridge, and I saw the blinking red light in the window of the Western Union Telegraph office. I didn't know what it did until much later, when I went to medical school. Then I came to hate what it stood for.

That is another story.

We soon passed the tenements and entered our town's small-business district. As we walked on, Papa would point out the different shops and tell me what they did and who ran them. We passed Mr. Ruddy's shoe repairs and Mr. Huff's electric motors. I smelled the ripe aroma of provolone cheese emanating from Mr. Zuppa's grocery and the pungent smell of hanging salami from the butcher next door. Papa didn't say much except that the butcher shop was owned by the Mad Russian.

"But Papa, why is he mad?"

"Just because, Berto."

Papa pointed out the radio-repair shop and told me that the man who fixed things there had actually worked for Mr. Marconi, the inventor of the radio, and his assistant was General Eisenhower's personal radio technician during the war that just ended.

We passed by the glazier (Are there still shops where you can get pieces of glass?), and then a storefront with a red-and-white-striped pole in front. A man even more stocky and muscular than Papa stood in the doorway.

As we moved on, a gruff, strangely accented voice called out, "Who cut kid's hair? I kill man who did that."

I saw Papa's fists ball up, and he turned and walked toward the man in the doorway. I yelled, "No, Papa," and the other man raised his arms, hands palm forward, and began to laugh.

Papa stopped and stared at him.

I got between them and looked up at the jowly-faced man wearing a short white jacket and dark pants. His solid-black hair was slicked down by pomade, and his eyes seemed peculiar in their shape. It wasn't until later, when I studied anthropology, that I learned about the tribes who had lived in the Steppes of Russia.

He looked my father squarely in the eye and said, "I am Putchenkov." He extended his right hand and Papa did the same. I relaxed when both men shook hands and my father replied, "I am Antonio Galen."

The other man winked.

"Was not Gallini?"

My father nodded and again the man laughed.

"Ya, they tried make me 'Putch.' I said I was not dog, and Putchenkov was good name.

"Now," and he looked down at me, "what is name?"

"Berto," Papa replied.

"Call me Thomas, Thomas the Barber."

"It's my birthday," I said.

"Ah, Berto, come in. I cut your hair!"

In those days, haircuts for men were twenty-five cents, thirty-five with a shave. Kids were ten cents. Papa shook his head.

"I cannot pay you."

"No, no. Is birthday gift."

To this day, whenever I enter a true barbershop for men—not those fancy, unisex salons and hair-stylist joints—the scents of bay run, lilac, allspice, and antiseptic trigger my olfactory memory of that day, when I first entered the shop of Thomas the Barber. Other scents I never learned to name emanated from the bottle-lined shelves on the mirror-covered walls. Shaving mugs, many of them personalized, hung from the back, and the small sink held the magical shaving soap and bristle brushes in a row. There were three, creamy-white, enameled pedestal chairs and six customer seats capped off by a table laden with issues of *Police Gazette* and *Grit*.

Mr. Putchenkov reached into a dark corner and pulled out a small, wooden, cushioned shelf. He placed it over the black leather seat, picked me up as if I were a feather, and sat me on the cushion. Then he draped a pinstriped, blue sheet around my chest and neck.

I kept looking at Papa, not knowing what to expect, especially when I saw Thomas pick up a big pair of scissors and a comb. He ran the comb through my hair, and suddenly I heard the snip-snip click, as the barber began to cut the shrub on top of my head.

Snip-snip click, snip-snip click. On it went, until my head actually felt lighter. He ran the comb through my hair then took another gadget, flipped a switch, and I felt the buzzing hum of the electric trimmer, as it moved up and down the back of my neck and under my ears.

When he stopped, he looked at me and asked, "You want shave?"

Papa laughed—again!

Mr. Putchenkov took a conical milk-glass bottle from the shelf and sprinkled a nice-smelling liquid on my head, massaged it in, then combed my hair back and said "done."

I looked in the mirror. Damned if I didn't look good!

Thomas turned to my father.

"When he need haircut, if he sweep floor that day, I do it. Okay to you, Antonio Gallini?"

They shook hands, and we left with me basking in the hair tonic Thomas the Barber had sprinkled on my head.

We walked a bit farther that sun-bright day and then slowly ambled back home. Mama saw us coming from the front window and waited for us at the top of the stairs. She stared at Papa in disapproval as we trudged in, but Papa's face, his wide grin lighting up the furnace-burnt darkness, stopped her. He put his arms around her, the way he must have done when I wasn't there, seemed to nibble on her ear and whispered, and then she giggled and smiled. She examined me, eyes sparkling, and said, "Bravo, Berto!"

What an amazing man Papa was!

I think of him now, when I see all the kids on medication to help keep them focused. If he were alive today he would have wrinkled his nose in disgust. I laugh to myself when I think of Papa and my first week at school.

When I started first grade, the teacher handed out workbooks. We didn't have a nun in that grade. I suspect our teacher was a newly minted member of the education community paying her dues in a religious school in a bad neighborhood.

I looked through the manuals for spelling, reading, and arithmetic. By the end of the first week I had filled them all out, front to back. The teacher had a hissy fit when she saw what I had done. She wrote a note to my parents and sternly instructed me to take it to them.

I took longer than usual to walk home that day, and then I waited a bit before giving the note to Mama. She read it and frowned but said nothing. Later, when Papa came home, she showed it to him, and he frowned, too.

And me? I was afraid—very afraid.

Mama and Papa said nothing to me.

Next day at lunch I almost peed my pants, when Mama and Papa both walked into the classroom. He was wearing his work clothes, so he had given up his lunch break to come to my school.

I heard the young teacher greet them, somewhat surprised as well. I heard her describe my crime of completing all my work the first week of school. And then I heard something wonderful.

"Teacher lady, why is this bad?"

It was Papa!

She stammered for a moment, as my father's eyes bored into her. This was no ignorant immigrant worker.

I am sure she is dead now, but I bless that young woman for having the common sense largely missing today, when she replied, "You're right, Mr. Galen. Let me see what I can do."

I hope God lets her know about my words of thanks. From then on, that dear woman brought in books from her own library for me to read, while the other kids did "Dick and Jane."

Maybe if I had been a schoolchild today I would have been classified as ADD, ADHD, or QRSTUV. On the other hand, my mind does tend to wander.

We were talking about the barber.

About every six weeks I would show up at Mr. Putchenkov's shop. There I would grab a broom handle—which was far taller than I was— and round up the piles of black, brown, blond, red, and gray-white hairs lying in clumps on the tile floor around each barber chair.

It used to remind me of the shaggy fur falling off the mange-laden dogs that wandered the neighborhood, often serving as large-sized cats when they chased down and ate the numerous rats living there.

It was a steamy-hot July day. The air was heavy, a mixture of various shop scents, musky male sweat, and stogie-smoking customers, all overpowered by the stench of whatever was decaying in the river. I had been sweeping for awhile but had to stop and catch my breath.

This was in the days before air conditioning, and even the black-enameled, reciprocating, metal-bladed fan did little to relieve the stifling humidity.

How did Papa manage to survive the foundry furnace heat?

"Here, boy ... Berto, sit."

The door to the shop was wide open, and assorted flies and other insects buzzed in to sniff the colognes and then fly out. There was no screen door, but somehow the insects didn't bother us. Maybe they recognized larger insects in the general scheme of life.

"Berto, you want Moxie?"

Thomas reached into a wooden icebox at the back of the store and took out two cold bottles of Moxie soda pop. Talk about ambrosia nectar!

Again, my mind wanders. Do they still make Moxie? I used to read the label, looking at the white-coated doctor/pharmacist staring out at me with a pointing finger telling me to drink Moxie for good health.

We sat there, Thomas sitting in one of his barber chairs and me next to a pile of *Police Gazettes*. He laughed and pointed at the top magazine.

"Lady got big bazookas there, boy."

The only bazookas I knew about were the ones used in the war, so what would a lady be doing with those? I just nodded.

"Mr. Putchenkov?"

"You call me Thomas, remember?"

"Yes, sir ... uh ... Thomas, how did you become a barber?"

"Why? You want to become barber?"

I had to admit that what he did seemed like fun: snip-snip click all day long. And this was before I met the lady under the bridge and began to hang around Dr. Agnelli's clinic.

"Maybe."

So many things fascinated me I barely had time to sleep. I spent a lot of hours at the library, too—by myself.

I know, I know. Today's social workers would have to rescue me, because they would have tagged my parents as neglectful for letting me run loose at such a young age—and, heaven forbid, at a library.

"Okay, kid, Thomas tell you life story. You know Mother Russia?"

I shook my head then said, "There's a big railroad there."

I had just read about the longest railroad in the world. Railroads fascinated me.

Thomas's face split in the biggest smile I had ever seen.

"Berto, I help build that railroad!"

He closed his eyes as he talked, and the little shop seemed to disappear, replaced by broad expanses of cold, open land.

"I born in Irkutsk, in Siberia, not far from beautiful lake—Lake Baikal. It twenty-fifth year of Tzar Alexander Nikolaevich Second."

By my reckoning that would have been 1880.

"My brother and me, twins. I better looking and stronger, but it good to have twin—no need for friends. We hunt, run, cut wood for Papa. We even walk to lake.

"When I thirteen I meet Maria Ivanova. You got girlfriend, Berto?"

I shook my head once more. I didn't want to mention Kate. Seven-year-old boys weren't supposed to like girls.

That, too, is another story.

He sighed. "She thirteen and have big bazookas, too."

He laughed, and then his face creased. I couldn't tell if it was sadness, anger, or both.

"Two years later Papa come to me and brother. He say son of Tzar, Nicholas Third, building railroad from St. Petersburg, capital city on western border of Russia, all way to Vladivostok in East—longest railroad in world! Papa said would be good jobs for two strapping boys.

"By then I love Maria Ivanova, want marry her. But Papa say go Lake Baikal. They start railroad bypass 'round lake. I leave. Brother promise to follow. Railroads big things back then. Even Prince Nikolas, later become Tzar, came. He declare railroad open.

"I cut wood. I help carry cross-beams for track. Muscles get big. See?"

He flexed his arm, and a football-sized bicep leaped out.

"I also freeze my…"

He paused. He realized he was talking to a kid and didn't want to get crude. It didn't matter. Even at that age I knew what he meant. Mine got cold when the heat didn't work in our tenement.

"No towns or pretty women, so hair get long. One day, other man hand me shears, tell me cut his hair. I cut. Terrible job. I cut more hair, get better."

His expression darkened.

"Make much money cutting hair—more than railroad work. Go home to Papa. Give him money then go see Maria."

His face fell, and his eyes moistened.

"You got brother, Berto?"

"No, Thomas."

"Good! You lucky. I find out Maria now live with brother. So I leave Irkutsk. Travel Europe, emigrate Canada. Go Vancouver, work as logger. Muscles get bigger. Cut more hair. Go San Francisco..."

"Why'd you come here, Thomas?"

He smiled but said nothing. Whatever it was, it wasn't pretty.

When we had finished our Moxies, he cut my hair. Then I swept the rest of the shop and went home.

A year passed. Every six weeks I showed up at his shop. We didn't talk about his family, but he did tell me more of his adventures helping to build The Great Siberian Railway—later called the Trans Siberian Railway and then just the Trans Sib. He described men freezing to death, getting crushed between railway cars, dying in fights, or being attacked by packs of wolves.

By then I was eight, and that's when the dead lady called me. Soon after that I knew what I wanted to do, what I wanted to be. I started hanging around Dr. Agnelli's clinic. But I kept showing up and sweeping up the barber shop, lulled by the snip-snip click of Thomas's scissors.

I was sweeping up one Indian-summer day. As usual the shop door was wide open, the flies buzzed, and the fan rattled in a vain attempt to cool off the inside.

That was the day I first saw the butcher.

He walked in, white apron stained blood-red to brown—old stains covered by new ones. He held a large meat cleaver in his left hand. He said nothing. He just sat in an empty barber chair and waited.

Thomas also said nothing. He finished with his last customer, walked quietly over to the second chair, took a straight razor from the shelf near the sink, pulled out the razor strop attached to the chair, and began to sharpen it.

The butcher clenched his cleaver more tightly.

Thomas took a mug down, put a bar of shaving soap in it, took a lathering brush, and applied the white cream to the butcher's face. As he brought the razor to bear on the man's neck, the cleaver rose for a brief second then settled down once more.

Thomas didn't even bother with the butcher's scalp. There was no hair there to cut.

When Thomas was done, the man rose from the chair, threw two quarters on the counter, and walked out.

Thomas looked at me. He winked, but said nothing. Then he cut my hair. I finished my sweeping and left.

Another year passed, and by then I was shadowing Dr. Agnelli's coat-tails at the clinic. One day it had been relatively quiet, with only a few knife wounds, sick kids, and a lady going into labor unexpectedly. I once had joked that he needed to stock some Moxie in the refrigerator, and by golly he went out and stocked it!

I was always amazed at refrigerators. Like the barber, Mama and Papa had an ice box that needed a new block of ice at least once a week. But a refrigerator? Wow! Just plug it in, and things got cold!

Anyway, Dr. Agnelli and I sat there in the back room on a thread-bare couch. He sipped a black coffee, and I luxuriated in a really cold Moxie.

Just then the outside clinic doors banged open, and loud shouts erupted. We ran to see a hysterical woman speaking in a foreign tongue followed by Thomas carrying the butcher in his arms. Dr. Agnelli immediately took charge.

"What happened?"

Thomas spoke quietly, but the tension in his voice was obvious.

"Chest. He clutch chest and fall."

Dr. Agnelli steered Thomas and his burden over to an empty gurney cart, listened to the man's chest, and then opened a drawer in the medicine cabinet and took out a brown bottle. He undid the cap, took out a tiny pill, and put it under the butcher's tongue.

Slowly, the man's hand, which had been tightly clutching his chest, relaxed, and the sweat on his forehead stopped its heavy dripping.

By then the nurse had wheeled in a big wooden box, a new toy of Dr. Agnelli's he had told me about a while back. She attached wide rubber bands with metal plates to the butcher's hands and feet and placed one plate on his chest.

Dr. Agnelli turned on the machine and watched, as a two-inch-wide strip of paper unrolled with black marks on it.

"See, Berto, this is what a man's life looks like."

He held up the strip, and I saw the peaks and valleys that graphed out the electrical energy of the heart. I didn't know it then, but the butcher's pattern wasn't good.

"Thomas," Agnelli called out, "is that his wife?"

"Yes."

"I need to speak with her. Will she understand me?"

"No."

"Will you translate?"

The barber nodded then motioned the woman over to where the doctor stood.

"Your husband is very ill. He has had a heart attack. He needs to go to the hospital. I can call for an ambulance."

Thomas spoke rapidly in the multi-consonantal language of his birth, and the woman started to shake and sob. He grabbed her by both arms and shook her, and she settled down. Again, rapid-fire words poured from his mouth, and finally she nodded agreement.

The hospital ambulance arrived shortly afterward. Not as fast as today's rescue squads, but in the end it made no difference.

That night, Nikolai Alexei Putchenkov, butcher, died.

Maria Ivanova Putchenkov became a widow.

And Thomas?

He went back to work.

Snip-snip click.

The Tick-Tock Man

There's always one—that kid who's slower than, not as sharp, not as coordinated as the rest of us. He's the kid who's picked last, even after the fat kid or the kid wearing glasses. He's also the one who stammers in class, his every effort to speak a constipation of mind and body.

Today we'd call him developmentally delayed or a special-needs child.

Kids are not as kind.

They'd call him a sped, a retard, a spaz, or just stupid.

The favorite name in my neighborhood was dork.

Even now I'm ashamed to admit that I joined in such ritual childhood torture, taunting kids who couldn't cut it, the ones at the bottom of the pecking order, something that seemed to construct magically without the aid or influence of adults.

That's when I met Paolo.

I was nine—that fantasy age of unlimited energy and curiosity. School had just begun, and there was a new kid in class, a new kid to our tenement neighborhood.

"Paolo Cherubini?"

Sister Concordia was our teacher that year. Her voice carried a musical lilt only the Irish can convey to their words. She called the attendance roll, asking us one at a time to stand and say our names.

Paolo stood up from the ancient, dark-oak desk with the hole in the top that once held an inkwell. He barely avoided falling over himself as he stood away from his chair, and then I felt my skin crawl as he spoke.

My old-man's memory recalls an olive-skinned boy, thin but with a head disproportionately large for his body. His mouth seemed set in a perpetual smile, lips a bit too large, eyes spaced not quite right, ears set slightly too far down. I had to look at him twice before the pieces of his face seemed to complete the puzzle.

After nearly half a century of dealing with the human machine and the toss-of-the dice results of chromosomal mixing I still cannot fit a label to that boy: fetal alcohol syndrome, in-utero infection, hydrocephalus, cerebral palsy variant, or a mixture of several of the nasties Mother Nature can play when She casts the genetic dice.

Even today the medical profession throws up its hands and just calls them "FLKs"—funny-looking kids.

Yes, doctors can be cruel, too.

He stood there, his arms moving back and forth. He opened his mouth and his jaw jutted forward.

"Uhhhh ... I-I-I-I am-m-m-m..."

And then he gulped and said "Puh-puh-puh-puh-puh-puh-p-a-a-a-l-l-l-l-lo Che-che-che-che-eru-bu-bu-bu-bu-bu-bino."

Thank God Sister Concordia was not like some of the other nuns. They would have forced him to say his name over and over, "until you get it right." Instead, she smiled and said, "Thank you, Paolo. You may sit down."

I saw other smiles in the class that day, but they were malignant ones, and I knew what would happen at recess.

"Hey, dork face, where ya from?"

Sammy Welch was mean.

Paolo turned toward him, that broad smile infuriating the other kid even more. Welch collected his hand into a fist to punch Paolo, when my friend Sal grabbed his arm and said "No!"

Welch pulled away and yelled, "Yeah, one wop protecting another!"

The next thing Sammy knew he was surrounded by my friends Angie, Tomas, Sal—and me!

But the recess-ending bell saved his ass.

No, we didn't make him one of the group—not really. We were too cool for that. But we did look after Paolo in the schoolyard and sometimes even walked him home afterward. It was hard not to feel sorry for him.

He was friendly like a puppy. He couldn't do enough for you, even though it wasn't what you wanted. I never saw him cry, even when kids like Sammy Welch snuck in a punch or tripped him when we weren't looking. I think our protection made Sammy even angrier and more determined to invoke pain.

It only stopped when Sal, the strongest of us, broke Sammy's arm. It was an accident, but it set in motion a series of events which, years later, culminated in a tragedy.

You see, Sammy's father, Samuel Welch Sr., was a cop and, unlike most of the decent, hardworking police at the time, a crooked one...

Well, maybe I'll tell that part of the story later.

On some Saturdays, when Angie, Tomas, and Sal had to "do things" instead of playing, I would contain my disappointment and meander around the neighborhood, shuffling my feet and trying to decide whether to hide out in Andrew Carnegie's library or keep going until I reached the end of the world.

Sometimes, when he saw me, Paolo would appear out of the

shadows of his building and tag along, puppy-like. I would talk to him—but not with him—and he would smile and smile, until I had to fight the urge to punch him myself.

One day he followed me for six blocks, away from our rat-infested enclave and into what everyone called the business district. That's where Harold Ruddy ran his shoe shop and George Huff owned his motor and electrical-repair business.

More about them later, too.

And there was an establishment that, even now, seemed incongruous to the neighborhood. It was a watch-and-clock shop.

No, it wasn't one of those fancy boutiques you see today, selling high-priced Swiss wristwatches and antique ormolu clocks. This one was a hole-in-the-wall. It was a run-down flea trap packed floor to ceiling with clocks and machinery and shelves holding boxes of parts and just plain stuff.

Inside that shop lived a hunchback gnome who also smiled all the time.

His name was Raphaele Buccinelli, but everyone called him Mr. Buck.

He was almost eighty when I first met him, and though it was quite a few decades ago, I still can hear his gravelly voice casting out bits of wisdom that have stuck with me like glue.

Walking past his storefront, door wide open to whatever insects hadn't deserted the neighborhood for better lodgings, I would yell, "Hey, Mr Buck, come on outside. It's a beautiful day."

From inside the smiling ogre would call back.

"Berto, if I do that people will see me sitting in the sun, half-asleep. They will say 'poor old man' and think there is nothing to be had here, and they will continue on down the street. No, Berto, I stay inside. Then people will think I'm busy, and they will think I am good."

He was right.

I found that out when I opened my practice many years later.

On this particular day, accompanied as I was by Paolo the human puppy, I called out, "Can we come in, Mr. Buck?"

Above the whir of motors and grinding wheels, I heard, "Yes, come in, come in."

I turned to Paolo.

"Mr. Buck is the man who makes clocks. Do your mama and papa have a clock?"

By this time we had worked out a system of headshakes and body motions on his part to eliminate the agony of his speech. He quickly nodded, and we entered.

Mr. Buck was in his workshop in the back.

We walked through the poorly lit room containing clocks on shelves, clocks hanging on the walls, and more clocks standing up against the walls.

We reached the cramped workroom, where tools of all shapes and sizes hung neatly from hooks on pegboard. I also recognized small lathes, pliers of all descriptions, inscribers, and more. Permeating the air was the mixed scent of machine oil and the distinct aroma of sweat and body odor that only the old exude.

I know that scent well now.

"*Ciao*, Berto! Who is your friend?"

When he spoke at length his Italian was different, an accent Papa later told me was Neapolitan. And there was something else I did not then perceive.

Before I knew it, Paolo had walked over to the old man, who was not much taller than he.

"Pup-puh-puh-paaaolo."

The watchmaker looked long and hard at the boy. Then he bent down and effortlessly picked up Paolo and sat him on a stool.

"Hello, Paolo. Listen, listen to the measure of life."

Tick-tock. Tick-tock. Tick-tock.

Oh yes, how could I have forgotten? The store literally vibrated from the army of escape mechanisms releasing gears powered by springs and pendulums, all tapping out in crazy-quilt cacophony the rhythm of existence.

Mr. Buck took the innards of a mantle clock from his workbench, set it in a brace, and put its pendulum in motion. We watched as each swing moved levers that in turn moved gears moving other gears moving more gears and finally the hands.

Paolo's eyes gleamed with an excitement I'd never seen before. He turned to the old clockmaker.

"T-t-t-t-tick-t-tock?"

"Yes, Paolo," he nodded.

The boy seemed hypnotized by the innards, but they were not the type of innards that interested me. I had already embarked by then on the path that would take me to medical school. Still, I was curious, too.

"Mr. Buck, how did you become a watchmaker?"

He leaned against the workbench, as Paolo kept tracing his fingers gently over the gears.

"Ahhh," he sighed. "I was never really good at anything back in the old country. I just missed the great wars with Mazzini and Garibaldi. I worked in the fields and knew that I would grow old, a hunchback good for nothing. So I ran away. I came to America in 1890."

He saw my jaw drop and laughed.

"Yes, Berto, I sailed across the Atlantic as a deckhand—on a boat with sails! When we landed in New York, I jumped ship."

He regaled me with his tale of standing in the middle of a street in the city, a horse carriage nearly running him over. Jumping out of the way, he spotted a sign attached to a lamppost. He said he had learned some English from books the captain had lent him out of pity.

"It took a while for me to translate it, but it was an advertisement for a school teaching the art of clock-making. I knew nothing about clocks, but it certainly beat hauling sails."

He said he walked twelve blocks to save the cost of a streetcar ride and arrived in front of a brownstone building. He climbed four flights of stairs and knocked on the door of the Black Forest Watch Repair Company. A heavy, German-accented voice answered and bid him to enter.

"Herr Vogelsong stood there," he said, "peering at me over iron-framed, pince-nez glasses. He picked up a piece of brass, put it in front of me, and handed me an engraving tool—a scriber. Then he uttered four words:

"'Draw a straight line.'"

Mr. Buck said he spied a straight edge lying on a nearby desk and reached for it. Almost instantly Vogelsong had grabbed it and smacked him across the knuckles.

"'Draw a straight line.'"

He said he felt stupid but finally realized what the man wanted. He held the brass block steady, took the scriber, and bore down. As he moved it across the soft metal, he could tell the line was far from straight, and soon he felt the sting of the straight edge again on his hand.

"I sat back and looked at him," he said. "He was smiling through his goatee and mustache. I stared at that block of brass, closed my eyes, and tried something I had never done before. I tried to focus myself.

"My right hand seemed to move of its own volition and when I looked down, there was a straight line!"

As Mr. Buck spoke those words, I saw Paolo's face lose its smile. He stared at the old man. Then he got off the stool, shook Mr. Buck's hand, and walked out of the shop without me.

I didn't see much of Paolo except in class after that day. He seemed quieter and didn't fidget as much. Angie joked that he must have found a girlfriend. This from a nine year old!

I had another one of those alone Saturdays toward the end of the school year, and once again I walked past the business district, waving at Mr. Ruddy, as he cut and shaped a new heel for a shoe. I smiled at Mr. Huff, as he turned the large lathe holding the rotor of an industrial motor to repair its coils.

It was still early—about seven-thirty in the morning—but plenty was already going on. Mornings served proprietors and customers well. This early in the day, the heat hadn't yet set off the odors of the tenements. And the doors stood open to the evanescent breezes that served as the only source of air conditioning back then.

When I came to Mr. Buck's shop, I had to blink as if to confirm what I saw: Now there were two gnomes sitting side by side at the workbench. Mr. Buck was one—and Paolo was the other.

I watched and listened, as the old clockmaker first pointed out different things and then observed, and the boy followed his directions. He smiled approval and Paolo smiled back.

I didn't understand, until a customer walked in and called, "Is this Raphaele Bachanale's place?"

Mr. Buck rose from his stool, came forward, and looked at the man.

"I am Raphael Buh-buh-buh-buccinelli."

Tick-tock.

The Coal Man

The coal man arrived one peppermint November day.

I awoke in the chill of a Saturday morning, the cast-iron radiator in my bedroom colder even than the air creeping through the cracks in the rotting window frame—nothing unusual for the decaying buildings in our neighborhood. Today one would call the city's housing office, and the bureaucrats would drag the absentee landlord downtown and threaten him with fines and court orders, unless he turned the heat on. But in those days the landlord stayed warm in his distant, well-kept neighborhood, fearing only the wrath of his demanding, overweight wife.

Mama and Papa remained in bed, enjoying the respite from work and the luxury of two bodies lying warm together under a patchwork, homemade quilt. But ten-year-old boys were driven by different instincts, and I was no different.

I had slept in my long underwear, having learned that my room would grow icebox cold. Then, in the morning, it was relatively easy to grab my worn, corduroy pants from the floor, slip them under the blankets, and slide my legs inside. A few minutes of shivering to warm both them and me, and I would proceed to the secondhand, argyle socks

Mama had gotten for pennies at the charity outlet in the church basement. Quickly checking my brown brogans to shake out any roaches wanting to set up housekeeping, I would shove my head into an outsized, pullover wool sweater. Now fully dressed, I was ready to face my world.

Most kids in my neighborhood, if they made it to adulthood, would remember the wonders of Saturday morning cartoons and serials at the neighborhood movie house. I never had the twenty-five-cent admission fee to the all-cartoon, all-morning shows at the Empire Theatre, so my weekend entertainment was self-made. I knew that Angie and Tomas, my best friends, faced the same predicament, and my first job was to hunt them down.

I savored the crisp air. My pre-pubertal body easily warded off temperatures that would send older folks shivering to the nearest heated building. But I was a kid, invulnerable and immortal. I never worried about the weather. So when I saw the steel-gray sky signaling the impending snow season, my only thought was that it would be a white Thanksgiving.

The marquee at the Empire touted the Saturday cartoon show. In less than an hour hundreds of kids would be lined up, pennies, nickels, dimes, and sometimes quarters at the ready, pushing and shoving to be the first to enter the maroon, velvet-lined movie house with its prized balcony seats. Where else could you watch a movie, chew gum, and throw spit balls, all for a quarter?

But for me this particular heaven was off-limits. So I whistled as I walked past, catching a glimpse of the name of that week's attraction emblazoned on a poster in the display window: "Sergeant York," starring Gary Cooper and Walter Brennan.

That was it! My mind raced and I began to run. Angie and Tomas also lived in tenements, four-story, sooty-gray, stone fronts that must have been nice a hundred years ago. Now they held the overflow of the refugees escaping war-torn Europe.

They saw me first and met me halfway down the block. We were twins ... no, triplets in appearance, our couture direct from church rummage sales and giveaways, the conscience-salving gifts of the well-to-do.

"Whadda we gonna do, Berto, hmmm?"

I grinned. Angie often tried to imitate Jimmy Cagney when he talked.

Tomas remained quiet. He was an overly thin kid, a follower who later got himself killed by following the wrong crowd. Come to think of it, so did Angie—but that's another story. He just found himself in the wrong place at the wrong time, when another kid's knife slashed his throat.

"The Old Guys are probably already putting away Rheingolds at Mr. Ruddy's. Bet their stuff beats anything at the Empire."

That was our name for the three elders who had fought in the Great War, friends who had left the confines of our neighborhood and enlisted in 1917 to fight the Huns: Harold Ruddy, George Huff, and Tim Brown.

Twice a week, they would meet in Mr. Ruddy's shoe-repair shop and relive old memories, killing off as many Rheingold soldiers as they could. And on the days when we had no school, chores, or other things like baseball to distract us, we would sit, wigwam style, on the floor and listen to the three recount their days of glory. Like most boys of the era, sometimes we picked up the empty brown bottles and let any remaining drops drain out onto our tongues.

Mr. Ruddy kept photos of himself on the walls—faded photos of him running for touchdowns in high school. He had been a tall, muscular boy, very handsome and no doubt a lady's man, with wide shoulders suitable even for a lineman topping a triangular torso and tree-trunk-sized thighs.

Now his thick biceps and powerful forearms propelled him around his machine-filled shop, and the first time I saw him my mind refused to accept the fact that there was nothing below his waist. His legs and most of his pelvis had become trophies of a German artillery shell. He used a specially cushioned, swivel stool and hand bars strategically placed in his shop and bedroom in the back to help him move—as well as a keen mind, a strong sense of ironic humor, and flashing blue eyes highlighting an always-smiling face.

It took me sixty years to understand.

We liked Mr. Ruddy, but we secretly made fun of him. It was hard for us not to make fun of Mr. Huff as well. He operated the only electric-motor shop for miles and was considered a marvel at all sorts of repairs. Friendly, honest and soft spoken, his picture also adorned Mr. Ruddy's gallery of honor.

Back then kids like us idolized baseball stars like Joe DiMaggio. But when we stared at the photo of the young George Huff, standing, bat in hand, the champion hitter of his 1916 high-school baseball team, we couldn't comprehend it was the same man before us. He had aged far beyond his time, his face drooping slightly to the right, a gift of shell shock and a severe concussion sustained in the trenches of Lorraine. I later learned that he never slept without awakening in screaming fits.

The third man, like Mr. Ruddy confined to a wheel chair, always tried to stand and shake our hands when we entered the shop. Mr. Brown was our neighbor. He lived in the tenement next door. He was younger than Mr. Ruddy and Mr. Huff—though only by several months—but the mark of time and the effects of German gas warfare had aged him in ways that the other men could only observe from a distance.

His sepia-tinted photo on the wall showed a slender, long-legged track star with shags of dark-brown hair cow-licking his forehead. Now we saw a sunken-chested, white-haired old man with scarred skin and labored breathing from almost non-existent lungs. Even the missing legs and wandering mind of his friends proved no match for the living death he endured: perpetual breathlessness, a near-suffocation that never ended.

It was to Mr. Huff's credit, and the friendship bordering on love among the three men, that twice weekly he would push Mr. Brown's wheelchair slowly down the street to Mr. Ruddy's shop. Often I wondered whether Angie and Tomas and I would be friends so much later in life.

Surviving them both by more than five decades, I still wonder.

The fourth Old Guy in the room appeared only by photo. The first time we stared at the picture-laden wall we saw four strapping boys—perhaps young men is more appropriate—standing close together in athletic clothes, arms interlocking across shoulders, smiling and staring out into an unknown future. When Mr. Ruddy saw us, he hoisted himself, monkey-like, onto the counter where he would place the repaired shoes for pickup by their owners.

"Boys, I know you're wondering, so I'm gonna tell you. See that other kid? That's Tommy Seidletz. The four of us signed up together, and together we all faced down the Huns in France. And at one turn or another, Tommy saved each of our lives."

He paused for just a second, and I thought I saw his eyes begin to water, but maybe it was just a trick of the light. Then he smiled, and those blue eyes flashed, as he raised a beer bottle in salute, and the two other Old Guys did the same. He spoke very quietly.

"Tommy took a bullet for me the day before my legs decided to walk away."

He looked out his storefront window and pointed.

"Boys, see that lady there?"

We looked. It was the Crazy Lady. Everyone knew her. White-haired, pushing a baby carriage with a watering can under a baby blanket, she walked up and down the street, stopping passers by and asking if they had seen her little boy. Even Papa knew her and would tell me at the dinner table always to respect her. She had lost a son in the Great War. And even in that neighborhood of want, the Crazy Lady never went without food or shelter.

Mr. Ruddy touched my shoulder. In a whisper he said, "That's Tommy's mother."

We sat for a while longer, as the Old Guys drank and reminisced. Their war stories always excited us and conjured up images of our charging a machine-gun nest or hurling grenades over barbed-wire barricades. But we were also ten year olds, and long attention spans were not our strong suit.

Mr. Brown saw us fidget, and he reached into his vest pocket, gasping out in his oxygen-starved and chemically scarred voice, "Here, guys, catch!"

Ah, the memory of us scrambling for those pennies makes me laugh even now. I still have mine. They were special pennies, with the head of an American Indian or an eagle in flight. It wasn't until much later in life that I found out they were collectors' items. I wonder what happened to Angie's and Tomas's pennies.

Mr. Huff took the hint and strapped Mr. Brown into his wheelchair. Then he picked up the empty bottles and lined them up like the dead soldiers that they were. When we were sure the men had finished with them, we picked up the bottles—worth two cents each at the local beer distributor—and headed out the door into the cold. Mr. Huff tucked a blanket around Mr. Brown's chest and wheeled him outside. Mr. Ruddy, ever smiling, waved goodbye to all of us.

Walking home, Tomas, who had been quiet all the while, suddenly smiled.

"Hey, guys, doesn't the coal man come today?"

I had forgotten about it. Maybe the numbing cold in my bedroom had frozen my brain. Sure, that's what happened! The building had run out of coal. It wasn't unusual. The only time owners paid attention to their tenements was when rents were due.

"Let's go! Maybe he's still there."

We ran across the bridge over the small river running through the neighborhood. Then we heard it: the groaning motor and grinding brakes of the big truck carrying tons of coal to fuel the tenement furnaces. It was stopping in front of my building.

We saw the big, soot-covered, glove-wearing man extend the metal sluice from the back of the truck. He walked toward a heavy, cast iron cover that concealed a chute into the basement. As we approached, he lifted the cover and guided the sluice from the truck into the opening. When he noticed us he flashed a gap-tooth smile.

"Stay back, kids, lotta soot gonna come out soon!"

His moon-round face reminded me of the members of the Polish family down the street.

Like magic we saw him pull a lever, and the back of the truck started to rise. As it did the thunderous hoofs of thousands of coal lumps funneled down the sluice and into the chute, colliding and bouncing and raising a thick plume. Despite his warning we got closer and cheered the black diamonds rolling downward.

Soon the moon-dark man pulled the lever again and truck's bed settled back down. He took a shovel and pushed the remaining pieces into the open chute then took a rounded-fringe broom and brushed the sluice. When he had finished he folded it back into the truck, climbed in, and waved to us, as he moved it to the next building.

Now it was nearing lunchtime, and each of us felt the rumblings in our guts. We waved each other away, yelling out that we'd meet later.

I ran inside, climbing the four flights of stairs and pushing open our apartment door. I remember the look on my mother's face: a mixture of disapproval, laughter and feigned horror at my sooty face and hands.

"Berto, go wash your hands and change your clothes—now!"

I went to my room and stripped to my long johns. I paused and looked out the window. Down on the street the coal man again was replacing the sluice onto his truck after finishing next door. Then he looked up and, to this day, I swear he saw me standing at the window and waved at me. He climbed into the truck and drove off.

Only minutes later, when I had put on relatively clean clothes and was heading toward the kitchen, I heard shouting coming from outside. My mother went to the window and opened it, and the voice of Mrs. Brown, Tim Brown's wife, shrieked in the cold air.

Mama ran to the living room, where my father was sitting, feet, propped up, and whispered in his ear. He stood up more quickly than I thought possible, grabbed his coat, and ran out the door. I heard his feet stomping down the squeaky stairway and the front door of the building open and slam shut.

I went to the kitchen and saw my mother sitting at the table, her head in her hands.

"Mamma, che ha torto?"

Mama, what's wrong?

She shook her head and said nothing.

In a little while I heard Papa's heavy steps, slower now, climbing the stairs. When he entered the apartment, Mama looked up at him. He shook his head.

"Il vecchio Signor Brown appena è morto."

Old Mr. Brown just died.

To this day I remember those words.

The memories they stir in me are a mixed and varied lot. By the time I was ten I had seen death in the knife fights on Hamilton Street.

I had even tried to help, to stop the outflow of the red river of life from those slashed and cut. But these were the deaths of strangers.

I knew Mr. Brown. I liked Mr. Brown. He was one of the Old Guys. And now there would be one fewer member at those meetings in Mr. Ruddy's shoe-repair shop.

Later in my life, my father's words from that day struck another chord.

He had called him "Old Mr. Brown." Back then, old meant someone in their forties, maybe even fifty. It was not usual for men to live too long, whatever that meant.

Old Mr. Brown wasn't more than forty-eight.

But, dear reader, there is one final memory, one that haunts me even now. Was it a trick of the imagination, an overactive ten-year-old boy's flight of fancy? Or did I really see it?

That moment, when the coal man looked up at me and waved, another person in his truck also looked up, smiled, and waved: Timothy Brown.

The 'Bo

When I was ten I wanted to run away from home.

Not that I was unhappy or mistreated—far from it. When I was ten I had gotten the wanderlust from listening to Thomas the Barber wax poetic about his worldly adventures after leaving Mother Russia.

I wanted to see places, places I could only read about in the Carnegie Library after school. In between sweeping out his shop, going to school, shadowing Dr. Agnelli at his clinic, and hanging out with my friends Angelo and Tomas—and sometimes Sal—I dreamed of foreign and exotic places.

I was Lawrence of Arabia, Marco Polo, Charles Lindbergh, and Admiral Byrd rolled into one.

Ta pocketa-pocketa-pocketa.

Just call me Berto Mitty.

Sometimes we would talk after visiting the Old Guys at Mr. Ruddy's. The tales they spun about "Gay Paree" and the battlefields of Europe put stars in our eyes.

It was Sal (Wasn't it always?) who suggested we go down to the railroad tracks. They were a bit of a walk, even farther than the rich people's neighborhood. We lived on the perimeter of a transportation hub.

New York City was to the northeast, and Elizabethtown Port was to the south. Both were far-away places. But the railroads ... ah, they lay right before us.

What boychik could resist the sounds and smells of the great metal beasts, the whistles and the clickety-clacks, as they pulled their burdens in and out of the vast rail yard just outside of Newark? What boy would not love the mixture of diesel oil, soot, and ozone, as both diesel-electric and coal-burning engines whooshed or roared past our perches along the edge of the gravel berm carrying the tracks to their respective terminals?

Whenever we were willing to walk the distance to reach the rails, we would sprawl out and watch. Freight trains, some a hundred-cars long, would roll over the multiple tracks leading in and out of the nearby industrial complexes that had sprouted up because of the war. Their giant, double locomotives let out their Doppler-shifting, banshee calls of greeting and warning as they passed each other. We would laugh and yell back "whoo-whooo!"

Sometimes an engineer, his arm hanging out the side window, would see us lying there. He'd wave and pull the cord of his whistle in greeting: "Awhooh, Awhooh."

In the other direction, behemoth, sleek diesel-electrics with insignias on them—Indian Chief, City of St. Louis, and others—pulled maroon coach cars filled with people reading newspapers or just staring out the window. Stainless steel and duralumin Pullman sleepers and dining cars, from places like Florida and Boston and points west, rumbled past, as each engine's single, giant, electric eye cast its light beam, even during the day, and the passenger trains slowed to enter the Newark terminal.

What could be more exciting and romantic for a ten-year-old boy than the snuffling of the wheels and the hissing of multiple air brakes?

"Hey, looka that guy! He just got pushed outta that freight car."

Angelo loved watching the freight trains more than the passenger liners.

Tomas yawned.

"Probably a 'bo."

Sal noogied Angelo's head.

"What's a 'bo?"

"He means hobo, Sal."

I was showing off my newly acquired book knowledge. I had spent a good part of the previous Saturday in the library. The black-and-white images of men during the Great Depression were still fresh in my mind—thousands of the economically displaced seeking their fortunes by riding the rails on the cheap, hitching aboard freight cars going anywhere but where they had been.

I still think of John Steinbeck's "Of Mice and Men." We stared at the patchwork man rolling down the steep track edge. He came to an abrupt stop in a stand of cat-o'-nine tails and sumac bushes and let out a groan. A cloth bag hurled out of the slowly moving freight car landed near us.

We were boys, and all boys, to put it bluntly, who grew up during that time thought nothing of walking at night and talking to strangers and playing rough-and-tumble games, all without some do-gooder yelling at your parents for being irresponsible or calling in the social workers.

Tomas, our Mercury, ran to the bag and picked it up. Angelo the trickster grinned and ran after him. He wanted to see what was inside the cloth pouch. I was startled when Sal yelled, "Leave it be! It belongs to the old man."

He ran toward the others. I followed.

"Come on, he might be hurt."

Sal took the bag from Tomas and approached the sprawled figure on the ground. We could hear his low moans as he twisted around before grunting and sitting up.

"You need help, Mister?"

"My bindle, where's my bindle. You kids got my bindle?"

Sal held out the bag, and the guy snatched it from his hand without a word. He untied the top string, rummaged inside, seemed satisfied that nothing was missing, and glared at us.

"You gonna help me up or not?"

We were taken aback. He saw our expressions, slapped his right knee, and started to laugh.

"Sorry gents, I forget my manners. Please, help me up. Okay?"

Sal stepped forward and held out his hands, and we followed suit. It took the three of us to get him to his feet, and even then he was a bit unsteady.

We could smell that hallmark combination of unwashed body, sweat, booze, and just plain rancidness. The guy's breath exuded stale tobacco and bad teeth. His face bore at least a week's worth of unshaved beard stubble and a mixture of old and fairly recent scars. The hands that we held hadn't seen soap or nail cutting for who knows how long.

But he laughed, as he tried to focus on all three of us at once. I noticed that one eye, his left, deviated out to the side. He patted the dust off his old, coarse, wool black trousers with button fly and then snapped his suspenders in place. The gray broadcloth coat he wore probably had been new sometime before World War I.

Tomas hesitantly asked, "Are you a 'bo, mista?"

Stretching to his full height—maybe five feet, nine inches—the man looked down at us and declared, "I am Mordecai Jones, late of Nova Scotia, Montreal, and points north. You may call me 'Professor.'"

"Yeah, right, you're a 'bo."

Angelo was not usually that blunt.

"Gentlemen, what are your names?"

We all hesitated then Sal spoke up.

"I'm Salvatore. These guys here are Angelo, Tomas and Berto."

"Ah, you're all *paisan*, right?"

That we understood. We nodded.

"Where do you live?"

We told him and he shook his head in disappointment—no easy pickings in our fun-filled little neighborhood. Then Tomas said, "But there are some nice places where you could get stuff."

He squinted at us and that left blue eye tried its best to accompany its brother.

"Have you seen anything like this in those nice places?"

He picked up a small stone from the track berm and squatted down. Then he began to scratch what looked like Egyptian hieroglyphics in the hard dirt.

They were symbols: ///, ##, and pictures that looked like a cat and a top hat with a triangle.

We all shook our heads at first, but then Angelo said, "Wait, I think I saw the cat in front of convent where the nuns live."

Mordecai Jones broke out in a grin, and we could see those stubs of rotten teeth jutting out.

"Whadda those mean, mista?"

Tomas was curious.

"They're 'bo signs, kid."

He turned to me then looked at Sal.

"Your friend doesn't say much, does he?"

"Be thankful, Mr. Jones. Normally he doesn't shut up."

It was true. I hadn't said anything. Watching Mordecai Jones, my wanderlust seemed to evaporate. My dream bubble had burst, and I did what I normally did when disappointment hit: I withdrew into silence. It wasn't until I was older, and my male hormones disrupted my sanity, that I was able to direct my anger and grief outward verbally. It didn't help fully, though, and even now I revert to the silence that speaks volumes.

"Watcha gonna do tonight, mista?"

Tomas was really on a roll.

"Yeah, you really need a bath, mister. You smell."

Angie wasn't holding back, either.

"Young man, get it right. I stink, you smell it. There's a difference."

We all nodded, and then I realized why he called himself "the professor."

"See that big tower over there with the long pipe hanging down?"

We looked up at the giant watering can. Behind it in the distance I could see the giant, neon, REDI-KILOWATT sign of Con Edison, and the Zipper Man sign.

"That's a water silo for the steam locomotives. I'll get my bath tonight when it's dark. Don't want to scare the ladies, do we, gents?"

When the others laughed, Mordecai noted my failure to join in.

"What's wrong, kid?"

"You."

My friends looked at me.

"Siddown, guys, let's see what's buggin' your friend here."

Three little Italian Indians sat in council around the 'bo, with me off to the side. He stared at me briefly then cleared his throat.

"You're a dreamer, kid, ain'tcha?"

Sal, Angie, and Tomas nodded vigorously.

"You wanna see the world, eh?"

I gave a silent nod.

"You will, son, just not my way. You got brains. That's what'll carry you away, not this," he said, waving his arms to encompass the rail yard.

Finally I spoke up.

"Why do you do this?"

I think I startled him. He remained silent a brief moment then grinned.

"'Cuz I want to, 'cuz I don't know anything else, eh?"

My friends and I sat quietly, until we heard a deep-bass shout.

"Hey, you, get away from them kids!"

Mordecai Jones muttered an "Oh, shit! It's the bulls."

He grabbed his bindle and jumped up.

"Gotta go now, guys."

He began a helter-skelter run across the tracks and around detached rail cars. We stood up as we heard the sound of heavy footsteps coming toward us. Three men approached in railway uniforms, wearing badges and holding Billy clubs and guns. I later learned they also were called "railroad dicks." They specifically kept watch over the yards and chased away—or punished—unwanted trespassers.

One breathlessly called out to us, as his two partners chased after the surprisingly fast-moving Mordecai Jones.

"That guy hurt you?"

We just shook our heads.

"Okay, that's good. But you don't wanna hang 'roun' here. You never know who or what you'll run into. Those 'bos'll talk yer ear off then steal yer last nickel. 'Sides, there's snakes 'roun' here."

The word "snakes" grabbed the four of us by the short hairs, and we sprouted beads of sweat. Sal let out a "thanks, mister," and we took off at a run back to the safety of our own little tenement world.

I never went back to the rail yard. Oh, I still love trains—the whistle howls, the locomotive sounds, the clickety-clacks and the swaying motion of the coach cars. Two of my favorite songs are Arlo Guthrie's "City of New Orleans" and Mack Gordon and Harry Warren's "Chattanooga Choo Choo."

Those are the romanticized views of rail life.

I cannot forget Mordecai Jones, the professor. During my medical training I saw many Mordecais brought into the emergency room— barely alive or just plain dead. Alcoholism, fights, the harsh reality of living on the road, all took their toll.

But sometimes, late at night, I hear the siren call of the rails, and I wonder: How did Mordecai Jones end his days?

A few Hobo signs:
/// - danger
- danger—site of a crime
0 ^ - rich people
cat - nice old lady who gives handouts

The Dove

Even in the chill of old age that long-ago October day haunts me still.

"Mama, Papa, can I go, can I go?"

I was almost eleven years old. Patience was still not a virtue.

Papa looked at me with one raised eyebrow then cast a glance upward at the woman he had loved since his childhood. Mama smiled and put her hand on Papa's shoulder.

"Desidera andare con il suo amico Giovanni ed il padre di Giovanni. Vanno guardare gli uccelli nella foresta."

He wants to go with his friend Johnny and Johnny's papa. He wants to see the birds in the forest.

Papa looked at Mama. No words passed between them, but it was understood.

He looked at me once more.

"Si, Berto."

I was going to visit a country farm with trees, birds, and other animals.

You might wonder, what was so special? Forests, trees, animals? Pretty tame stuff for most, but growing up in my neighborhood, where the nearest thing to plants were weeds struggling to survive in the cracks

of decaying concrete, and where the only birds were the pigeons bob-
bing along the sidewalks and roosting in coops on the roofs of the tenement buildings.

Well, it seemed pretty damned special to me.

I still recall Papa opening the warped front window to our apartment and placing the remaining crusts of his bread on the sill. The pigeons would land in twos and threes, stare at him briefly, and gobble up
what he should have eaten. Some even allowed him to stroke their
heads.

Mama would smile when I asked her why Papa did that.

"Berto, your Papa and I, we came from the village."

That was all she said, but I understood. Mama and Papa had crossed
an ocean in early 1914, leaving their tiny village to escape the guns of
war and find opportunity in the gold-lined streets of America.

Strange, even now I often lay in bed and wonder: What would my
life have been like in their village?

I cannot even imagine.

I had met Giovanni in school. His real name was John, but we called
him Giovanni, and he seemed to like it. His father worked at the metal
foundry like Papa did, but Giovanni's dad was the manager. He didn't
go near the furnaces. He also got paid a lot more.

And Giovanni's dad had a car!

During the war, many things we take for granted today were scarce:
meat, soap, even toothpaste. Scarcest of all were cars, tires, and the
gasoline to power them. Giovanni's dad was the manager of a critical
war-industry factory. The foundry produced heavy-duty tools needed
to build the ships and planes we hurled against Tojo and Hitler. Most
other people could only buy as much gasoline as their ration cards per-
mitted, but Giovanni's dad could buy as much as he wanted.

Giovanni's dad was an important man. He owned a house in town, but he also had a farm far from the urban decay, and even the farm was considered important to the war effort.

My friend Angie was the first to meet the new kid. We all went to the Catholic school located between our neighborhood and the well-kept, rich people's enclaves. The nuns were the only ones who could maintain a semblance of order over us. Hooded and unflappable, the women who could stare down neighborhood toughs ruled the classrooms with iron fists—and a heavy ruler they sometimes fiercely applied to the open palms of those who failed to pay attention or study their Baltimore Catechism.

"Hey, kid, where you from?"

Angie had no fear of confronting someone new. Oh, he'd run from trouble, but facing another kid to gauge where he would fit into the pecking order? That was no sweat.

It's also what got him killed four years later.

"My dad just got transferred to the foundry here. We used to live in Pennsylvania."

He named a town that I later learned was famous for coal and steel production, but back then it meant nothing to me.

Angie persisted.

"Whatcher dad do?"

Angie's dad, like mine, worked at the foundry. He was a big man, taller than Papa but not as strong. He drank himself to death after Angie was killed.

The new kid hesitated. I think he was actually embarrassed.

"He's the plant manager."

Angie's eyes widened. No, he wasn't afraid of the kid. Angie could always spot a hidden opportunity. If he had lived he would have put Sergeant Bilko to shame.

"Whatcher name?"

"Johnny."

"Naw, yer one o' us, now. It's Giovanni."

Far from being taken aback, the new kid grinned, as Angie corralled him with an arm across his shoulder and introduced him to the rest of us.

"This here's Tomas, he can really run. And Sal—hey, Sal, show Giovanni here your muscles."

Yes, Tomas could run. Thin as a rail, he could run like the wind. But he couldn't outrun the bullet that cut him down when he was sixteen. And Sal, he became a neighborhood enforcer. It took a drive-by shooting and multiple wounds from shotgun blasts to kill him on his twentieth birthday.

Then Angie pointed at me.

"This here guy is Berto. He talks a lot and likes to read, but don't let that bother ya. He's really good to know if you ever get hurt."

I laugh at that now. Yes, I was *Dottore* Berto to my friends and the neighborhood toughs. But when those closest to me were mortally wounded, I couldn't save them.

I laugh now, but tears soon take over.

Giovanni and I got along right from the start. He liked to talk about his home back in Pennsylvania and his friends there. He also liked to read, and when we weren't batting a ball around in the paved lot behind the Greek Orthodox Church with the other guys, the two of us would hide out at the library.

Strange, when I think of the old Greek church, just a block away from my grammar school, the aroma of pirohis and incense come to mind. And the library, at the very edge of our neighborhood, casts an olfactory memory of furniture polish and musty paper. For me those scents were the finest perfume in the world.

The little brick building at the crux of Hamilton and Eastep was incongruously well kept, one good tooth set within the rot and decay.

The oval, concrete silhouette of the robber-baron steel magnate stared down at us from the lintel of the big oak doorway. We would laugh at it and stick our tongues out, never realizing that the man who sought redemption and immortality by bequeathing libraries had once been the poorest of the poor.

That library became our sanctuary, our magic carpet to other lands, other times. On bad-weather days, it sheltered us from the elements, as we read and looked at pictures of sun-filled shores.

And Giovanni and I talked.

I let him do most of the talking—unusual behavior for me. I listened, as he spoke of the dairy farms with hundreds of cows not far from where he once had lived. And then, almost in non sequitur, he said, "Wanna see it?"

I was caught off guard. Yes, me, I was suddenly speechless. I tried to cover my lack of understanding by scratching myself—a guy thing, but it works among guys. Then I bluffed.

"You don't mean…?"

"Yeah, my dad was talkin' about going birding back at our farm next weekend. It's dove season. Wanna come with us?"

He really wanted a friend, and even though his dad was Papa's "big boss," I liked the kid.

"Uh, yeah, but I gotta ask my papa if I can go."

And that was it. The plan was to leave Friday evening, drive to Pennsylvania, and come back Sunday evening. All I had to do was persuade Mama and Papa to let me go.

"Berto, you will have to finish all of your homework first."

Mama wasn't sure about me being away for two days, but I didn't retort with what I was thinking: She had crossed the Atlantic Ocean with Papa to come to America, when they were barely fifteen and spoke almost no English.

Papa looked at me. I wore a big brass buckle on my belt with my name on it that he had made for my tenth birthday. He had called me a man then. I wanted him to see it, to remind him of what he had said. I was sneaky.

"*Figlio mio*, what will you do there?"

He knew who Giovanni's dad was. He was the Big Boss, the one who could fire a man on a whim.

"Papa, Giovanni says his dad goes birding, and there are doves there. I guess we'll be looking at birds and walking around the farm and the woods."

I didn't tell him that "birding" and "dove season" meant nothing to me.

Papa nodded. I don't think he understood, either.

That's how it went all week, until that Thursday evening when he finally said, "*Si, Berto.*"

School on Friday seemed to last forever. I just missed being the target of Sister Grace Roberta's wooden ruler and heavy hand. Sal was more restless than I was, not an unusual event, so her attention fixed on him. He stood there while she delivered her usual withering comments on his behavior and intellect, throwing in a few opinions about his immortal soul, then told him to open up BOTH hands. This was highly unusual.

Sal grinned, did as he was told—palms up—and turned his head toward me and the other guys. I can still hear the "whap, whap, whap" of those smacks on his skin. I saw his eyes dilate, constrict, then return to normal.

It wasn't until I was in high school that I understood the body re-flex that caused it to happen. All I could do then was focus on his eyes. Those large, dark, almost-black irises that later attracted the girls and instilled fear in his enemies—constricting, dilating, constricting.

The only other time I saw Sal's eyes dilated like that was when he lay dead on the sidewalk in front of the pizza joint that served as a meeting hall for the Sicilianos and their enforcers. He wasn't smiling then. I saw Sister Grace Roberta praying at his funeral.

But on that day Giovanni was excited and restless, too. We both managed to make it to the three o'clock school bell then ran like hell out the door to the school playground.

I had brought my bag—literally, a paper bag—with clean underwear. Mama had yelled at me, when I said I should be able to wear what I had on for almost three days.

Mothers are girls, so they don't understand how guys think.

We waited about twenty minutes and then saw Giovanni's dad's car pulling up on the side street. I had never seen a car so nice. It was a 1937 Chevrolet Master Deluxe sedan with running boards and tire guards that today remind me of the nacelles on jet planes.

Giovanni told me to jump on the right running board, and he did the same on the left, while his dad drove about a block down the street then stopped. He was laughing at our antics and, no doubt, we looked like little monkeys hanging onto his car. At that moment all three of us were boys.

I wonder if kids today have as much fun.

I am embarrassed to admit that I briefly wished Papa could have been fun like Giovanni's dad. Why is it we have to learn by experience what should be so obvious?

Cars didn't have seat belts then, or collapsing steering columns, or air bags, either. The front windshield was two panes of flat-plate glass with a metal seam in the middle. Together the car's features made quite an array of potentially lethal weapons.

Giovanni and I took turns jumping from the front seat to the back, while his old man drove the wartime-mandatory 35 miles per hour along the back roads of New Jersey, finally reaching the Pennsylvania border and the almost-brand-new stretch of the Pennsylvania Turnpike.

It took four hours, and by the time we left the 'pike dusk had arrived. The twin, bug-eyed headlamps did little to light the darkness of roads without lights.

Another two hours and the pavement became gravel and rutted. Then we pulled inside a whitewashed fence up to a farmhouse in the middle of nowhere.

Giovanni's dad walked to the front porch, opened a storage bench, and took out a kerosene lamp. A quick strike of a lucifer and the flame illuminated the surroundings enough for us to find our way inside. His father threw some pieces of chunk coal into a cast-iron stove, put some kindling inside, and another lucifer soon had the coal glowing just right.

It was an apple-butter October night, the cool Pennsylvania air carrying smoky scents from distant farmhouses, and the only light cast from a partially clouded, quarter moon.

"Hey, Berto, don't let the bats scare ya."

Giovanni leered at me, as we climbed the ladder to the house loft where we would sleep. The faint moonlight through the window outlined a single bed just big enough for two preadolescents to jump up and down on and wreak general havoc, until they fell asleep.

I never slept so well at home. It wasn't until I was older and visiting the family farm of my medical-school roommate that I re-experienced that same, deep slumber.

I laugh now at the thought. We slept deeply, because we were young boys with no worries.

Giovanni showed me the outhouse next morning, and even though I was used to seeing insects in our apartment, I never had to worry about snakes and other, unnamed creatures keeping me company while relieving myself. I fought my natural inclinations and did not run screaming out the door with the little half-moon cut into it.

The cold water from the hand pump braced me for what Giovanni's dad had fixed for breakfast: cooked eggs he had brought from New Jersey, sourdough bread, and the most godawful-tasting chicory coffee—real coffee being another war-shortage commodity.

Giovanni put on a bright red jacket and lent me another one to wear, along with a red hat to cover my head. I asked him why the red, and he matter-of-factly said it was to prevent us from getting shot.

Getting shot at was not exactly something new to me. It went on all the time down on Hamilton, where the different ethnic territories converged. But I didn't expect that type of activity around here, on an isolated farm. Then I saw his dad unlocking a tall cabinet and taking out a shotgun—a side-by-side, double-barrel, twelve-gauge—and a box of shells.

"Come on, guys," he said. "We're heading out to the blind."

I didn't say anything. It was all new to me, and besides I didn't want to look foolish. I followed Giovanni out the door. The gun was empty, but his dad still carried it in the open-breech position with the barrels open and hanging down, a habit meant to prevent an accidental discharge in case of a fall.

We walked through a nearby copse of trees. Giovanni told me his dad had planted them to act as a windbreak against storms.

The trees soon gave way to an opening onto a large, grassy field. We stopped at the opening, and his father whispered for us to keep quiet. Then we moved about twenty feet into the tall field grass, to a place the man called the "blind," a fort-like semicircle of stones that allowed us to sit and not be seen from the rest of the field.

"Okay," he said, pointing. "The doves make their nests over there near the tree line. Son, when I tell you, hurl that fallen branch as far as you can in that direction. It oughta flush them out. I'll take the first shot, then I'll let you do it."

He took two shells from the box, loaded the shotgun, and closed the breech.

I turned to Giovanni.

"What's your dad going to shoot?"

"Doves, what else? I told you it was dove season."

It finally hit me: We were hunting. We were going to kill doves.

"Okay, Johnny," his dad whispered. "Throw the branch."

Giovanni flung the piece of dead tree back toward the woods. As soon as it landed, a flutter of wings rose from the ground, and gray-brown and whitish pigeon-like birds filled the sky like large, multihued snowflakes—life rising to meet the heavens.

Now the heavens reciprocated with death. The shotgun blast reverberated once, and I saw several birds plummet back to earth like bombs out of a B-29 Superfortress.

Giovanni's dad quickly reloaded the shotgun and handed it to his son, who raised it at the remaining flying creatures circling overhead. He fired.

I have several images of that scene embedded in my mind: the falling objects, those once-living creatures, their beaks hanging open, and their wings motionless; the proud look on the face of Giovanni's dad, and Giovanni himself, his legs spread in wide stance, the shotgun taller than he was held in his conqueror's hand.

"Let's go get our dinner."

I stood there, unmoving, as father and son fanned out, picking up the dead birds and stuffing them into a sack. Then I heard Giovanni.

"Hey, Pop, this one's still alive!"

His dad moved quickly toward him and took the bird from the boy's outstretched hand.

"All right, son, watch carefully. It's real easy. Grab the head here, twist and pull at the same time. Just like taking a cork out of a bottle."

It was fast, but I saw it as if in slow motion. Giovanni's dad gave the creature's head a sudden twist and pull, and it popped right into his left hand, the neck and body remaining in his right.

"Wow, Pop, that's neat!"

Giovanni became so excited he nearly jumped up and down.

They continued picking up birds, and then Giovanni called to me.

"Hey, Berto, here's another live one. Wanna try it?"

I walked over to him and saw the bird, its chest still rising and falling rapidly, its left eye seeming to stare out toward where its nest was. Giovanni grinned, grabbed its head, and performed the simple maneuver his dad had just taught him.

I stared at that head and watched the eye facing me slowly dilate then cloud over in death.

"Here, Berto, catch!"

He laughed as he threw it at me.

I caught it easily and stared at it then turned and walked back toward the woods. I heard Giovanni call, "Watch out for poison ivy!"

I found a spot under a tree where the ground was soft and easy to disturb with another fallen tree branch. I dug a hole, placed the dove's head in it, beak pointing toward its nesting site, covered it with dirt, and placed a moss-covered fieldstone on top. I kept walking in what I thought was the direction of the farmhouse and, after a short while, it came into view. I sat on the porch bench, watching the tree sparrows and blue jays land on the pump handle and stare at me as an outsider. I could hear the echoes of more shotgun blasts.

I must have fallen asleep. I found myself being shaken, and I looked up to see Giovanni pushing my shoulder.

"What happened to you? We thought you had gone in the woods to take a piss, but when you didn't come back we started to look for you. Pop wanted to teach you how to shoot the shotgun."

I knew I couldn't tell him the truth. This called for what I later learned was termed a "white lie." I smiled weakly at him and said the chicory must not have agreed with me—that I had "the trots."

Giovanni seemed to understand and said he didn't know how his dad could drink that crap. I laughed weakly.

The rest of the day we wandered around the farm, while his father cleaned and dressed the day's kill. That evening I begged off eating any of the birds. I just munched on more sourdough bread to "settle my stomach."

Sunday morning, Giovanni's dad stuck his head up in the loft while we were still in bed and said we had to leave early. He had gone into the local town to call the foundry and was told he needed to return right away.

Giovanni was disappointed, and I faked feeling the same. He said he had wanted to teach me how to hunt.

We left an hour later.

Giovanni invited me once more to his farm, this time for deer season. I lied and said Papa wouldn't let me go because he had work for me to do.

That weekend passed quickly, and I expected Giovanni to come by when he got home. No one showed.

I went to school Monday, and none of us saw him.

Then Papa came home from his shift at the foundry. He couldn't look at me. He went into the bedroom and Mama followed. I heard her gasp. They both walked back out, and Papa told me to sit down at the table. He looked at me then lowered his eyes. Mama put her hand on my shoulder, as Papa spoke.

Giovanni and his father had been killed in an auto accident. They were driving back home from their farm, when a deer bounded into the road. Its antlers entered the car through the open, driver's-side window. The car swerved and crashed into a tree, throwing Giovanni through the windshield. The antlers had decapitated his father.

I have seen many things since then. I have seen life enter the world and death take it away. In the name of self-defense, I have even assisted death, both as civilian and on the battlefield. But in the winter of my own life, I remember that October day, the day I stared into the eye of a dying dove, and I wonder: In their last moments, did the eyes of Giovanni and his dad look the same?

The Candy Lady

Daddy, do you love me?

Of course I do, dear.

Would you jump off a bridge with a defective bungee cord for me?

You know I would.

Daddy, would you get a colonoscopy?

Uh, kid, I think I hear your mother calling you.

OMIGOD!

Sister Mercy Grace was going to give me a colonoscopy!

Well, not really. It wasn't "Sister No," as we had nicknamed her in seventh grade. But the young, colorectal surgeon sitting behind her desk for my pre-colonoscopy interview sure as hell looked—and acted—like her.

Only those who have not suffered the indignities of frequent prostate checks, mammograms done by Ernest and Julio Gallo, and engine tune-ups with stents in the heart, can claim that old age grants dignity. And for those of us over fifty—in my case way over fifty—

there is the ultimate degradation: having the privilege of lying naked and unconscious on an operating table with one's butt exposed to amuse and bemuse the OR staff.

What follows is the piece de resistance. That involves having a length of fiber-optic garden hose jammed up the rectum and into the colon like a perverted plumber's snake. All this after doing a "bowel cleansing" that would make water-boarding seem like a visit to a massage parlor.

Regarding massage parlors, as in so many other lightly touched-upon topics, that is yet another story.

The only good thing is that you are unconscious—or supposedly so—after having a large-bore needle jammed into a vein in your hand and seeing the lights go out with a gentle push on the syringe that contains the knockout drugs.

So, there I sat with my ward, Antonio Hidalgo. He had convinced me that the off-and-on aches in the left-lower quadrant of my abdomen should be checked out.

Lest you think that doctors are smart and courageous regarding their own health, especially one who is approaching eighty, let me dissuade you of that illusion. Doctors are, by nature and by training, big chickens when it comes to having procedures performed on them.

My doctor was tall and well-proportioned, her white lab coat the opposite of Sister Mercy Grace's black habit. But like the good sister, she had piercing eyes shielded by round, wire glasses, and her voice echoed a Gaelic ancestry. She looked at me as a relic of past medicine, but she was courteous and relatively straightforward in her discussion of what was, to me, nothing new. I understood the risks of the procedure. As a young resident I actually had worked with some of the pioneers in fiber-optic scoping of the GI tract.

I had brought Tonio with me for several reasons. One, I needed a driver. I no longer trusted myself to get behind the wheel with the incipient cataracts developing in my eyes. Another was the boy's—I should say young man's—interest in medicine as a career.

Antonio Hidalgo was the youngest of three Cuban boat children my friend Edison and his wife Nancy and I had rescued years before. Now, Tonio was approaching a decision point in his life. He was a junior in college, and the time for medical school applications was drawing near.

The boy was not my genetic stock, but he was as close to being a son to me, in both temperament and ability, as any sperm-egg union could have produced. An old man seeks immortality through his children, and that boy would carry on my life's work. I had taken him on rounds, and the kindness of my colleagues had exposed him to what life as a doctor would be like in different medical and surgical fields. Now it was up to him. Would Apollo's son Aesclepius grant him entrance into the healing arts?

As the pre-procedure interview drew to a close, I looked directly at the young doctor and asked a favor.

"May Tonio suit up in scrubs and observe the procedure you'll be doing on me?"

That's when the voice of Sister Mercy Grace echoed down through the years, as she assaulted my ears with a loud and very emphatic, "No!"

Yes, I wanted him with me, but not only to observe and learn. I admit that my fear of the partially known also drove that request.

Age has smoothed the rough edges in my volatile temperament. I was initially shocked by the seemingly irrational reply. My mind scanned the potential reasons why she would refuse a colleague's simple request. And being temperamentally volatile I fought for control by pressing my fingernails into my palms. I would not be angry or confrontational. Neither would I beg in front of my adopted son. I explained Tonio's background and interest in a medical career, and his prior experience in hospitals and ORs. It made no difference.

I said nothing as she scheduled the procedure time, and then Tonio and I left. I said nothing as he drove me back to Safehaven, my adopted home in the north-central mountains of Pennsylvania. He looked at me from time to time but had the wisdom to remain silent.

That night I sat in my study trying to distract myself by reading some recent medical journals. I must have fallen asleep at my desk

Did I dream, or was what happened next a memory?

"Sister Mercy Grace may I be excused?"

My friend Salvatore—always Sal to me—was already in the throes of puberty and was somewhat out of place by seventh grade. The rest of us were barely noticing the soon-to-be devastating changes wrought by surging levels of previously non-existent hormones. But Sal? Well, he already sported a five o'clock shadow—and this was 8:30 a.m.

Poor kid. He was built like a rock but nevertheless experienced loss of bladder control from his drunken father's numerous kicks to his abdomen as a young child. And when Sal actually sounded polite as he raised his hand—no antics, no smiles—we knew he was hurting.

Sister Mercy Grace stared at him, a mere larva in her scheme of things, and pronounced sentence.

"No!"

To this day I will swear on my parents' graves that an ephemeral smirk crossed her face.

God bless Sal. He said nothing. He arose, walked to the classroom exit, turned around once to give that woman a look that sent shivers down our spines, and then opened the old mahogany-stained door and left. The hooded she-devil called his name once then smirked again, as she picked up her ruler and waited.

We held our breaths.

Less than three minutes later he returned, legs uncrossed, and walked past Sister Mercy Grace's desk.

"Salvatore, come here."

He turned to look at her once more, and this time we all knew—it was war. He continued to his desk and squeezed his muscular body into it. He looked up at her but said nothing. Then, still focused on the nun, he picked up a thick black pencil, held it in one hand, and easily snapped it in half.

She put the ruler down and started lessons for the day.

It wasn't over.

From then on nothing Sal did was right. Whatever he did, whatever he said, it was wrong. It got to the point that the entire class—after hearing him answer her question correctly and then being scolded for being wrong—actually hissed the black-habited tyrant under our breaths. Numerous hands, including mine, felt the sting of that damned ruler—but not Sal's. She was lucky that Sal, despite his size and great strength, was the gentlest kid in class.

That afternoon I witnessed something surreal. Sister Mercy Grace stood in the hallway after school, and one of our prior teachers, Sister Grace Roberta, was engaged in an animated conversation with her. I liked Sister Grace Roberta. She was strict but had always been fair. Now I saw her become highly agitated with a fellow nun to the point of shaking her finger in the taller woman's face. It was only the site of my friend Angie and me walking down the corridor that stopped Sister No from striking the much shorter Sister Grace Roberta.

Eight years later I finally learned why that wonderful doll-sized woman had become so involved in "L'Affaire Salvatore."

Need I say it? Another story.

Seventh grade wasn't all whacks with a ruler. Catholic grammar schools—in their great wisdom—separated the boys from the girls in what is now called junior high. Each had his or her own homeroom. It was an attempt by the celibates to control the rising libidos of their charges. It didn't really stop guys from noticing the developmental changes in the girls who had shared a classroom with them before seventh grade. It also didn't stop the girls from noticing the boys grandstanding out on the playground—all calculated to impress the strange new species that had evolved from former tomboys. Both sides stared at how the other filled out formerly flat blouses and/or slacks.

I was no different.

I had my eye on a couple of the "chicks" who used to hang out with Angie, Tomas, Sal, and me before the pubertal putsch. And then I saw the new girl: She was stunning!

To this day, now bordering on the edge of becoming plant food, I fondly remember Bernice—Bernice Johnson. Long-legged tall, she could run almost as fast as Tomas. Her face like Nefertiti, she flashed a smile lit up by porcelain-white teeth and sparkling brown eyes, and she could outtalk Angie.

Of course, it was her mind that attracted me. Yeah, right.

No kidding, that girl could get me into near-violent debates on just about anything. Neither of us won—we always battled to a draw—though I suspect she could have bested me easily. But she exercised that amazing sorcery all women have, and which more than a few choose to use, and she would let my ego remain unbruised and let me think I had gained the advantage.

Oh, I forgot to mention, Bernice Johnson was, as the politically correct say today, an African American. Every time I see a shimmering, golden-brown piece of Godiva chocolate, I still think of that gorgeous, unbelievably talented girl.

As my father would say when he talked about seeing Mama for the first time, I "had the horn" for Bernice.

I was lucky. She had to walk home each day past my apartment building, so I always managed to be out on the sidewalk at the same time. My friends teased, but I had seen the pairings off of Angie and Yvette, Tomas and Monica, and even bewhiskered Sal and Cynthia, so it really didn't bother me.

My neighborhood was a hotbed of ethnicities, each with its own un-
written but well-delineated territory: Italians, Eastern Europeans,
Greeks, some scattered Central and South Americans, and African
Americans, all within spitting distance of one another. You had to be
careful where you walked, although my reputation as *Dottore* Berto
allowed me entrance and egress without interference.

I had it all figured out. Bernice had to walk past some of the small
shops just outside the tenement complexes. One in particular fit my
scheming little mind: old Mrs. Donnelly's candy store. That's where I
could really impress her.

But first I had to consult my *consiglieres*.

Primo consigliere: Mama.

"Mama, can I ask you a question?"

She was sitting in the old rocker that once had belonged to Mrs. Fla-
herty, the boarding-house owner who had taken in Mama and Papa
when they arrived from Ellis Island. On her deathbed from the pan-
demic flu the old landlady had given it to Mama. Now she was quietly
darning the constantly appearing holes in Papa's and my socks and
pants.

I must admit, just like any early adolescent, I was reticent to talk
about my budding courtship. Oh, it wasn't that Papa and Mama—especially Papa—hadn't talked to me about girls and … well … you
know. I was a typical thirteen-year-old boy.

"*Si*, Berto?"

I think she knew. Mama and Papa had spotted Bernice and me one
day just hanging out on the steps of our tenement, and when I entered
our apartment both showed those embarrassing, all-knowing grins that
tell you they have deduced your secret.

"Uh…"

I was still grasping for the right words and the courage to speak.

"Mama, how did Papa impress you? Did he give you flowers or candy or what?"

I actually blushed from her gaze. Then she rose and threw her arms around me, rocking me like she had done when I was little and had stubbed a toe.

Then, after emitting a memory-inspired sigh, she whispered in my ear.

"Your Papa saved me from the cows!"

She smiled, her rounded face lighting up from that recollection, and then delved into my soul.

"Berto, what is her name?"

I stared down at the floor.

"Bernice," I stammered.

"Is she nice?"

"Oh, yes, Mama! And she's smart and a fast runner and..."

She put her index finger on my lips to stop the outpouring then reached into her apron pocket and took out three pennies.

"Here, Berto, a girl always loves candy."

I hugged Mama and ran outside.

Next stop, Dr. Agnelli.

I headed to the free clinic run by my mentor. My legs were lengthening now, along with the rest of my anatomy, and running had become far easier than when I was younger. I didn't even get winded. I opened the big glass door and was greeted by the nursing staff with whistles and "Hey, Berto."

Truth be told, I was pretty damned good-looking as a teen.

Dr. Agnelli had just finished with a little boy who had supposedly fallen down the stairs and broken his arm. He wasn't smiling.

"Mrs. Pesca, are you sure Ignatio fell?"

He stared into the tremulous woman's eyes and saw the resolving bruises in the whites and fresh bruises on her arms and forearms.

He turned to me, and I knew that look. He was angry—not at me or the woman or her son, but at her wife-beating, child-abusing, common-law husband who had done this. He reached for the phone, and as the rotary dial whizzed and clicked out its connecting signal I recognized the number of the local police.

Mrs. Pesca jumped up and pressed the handset bar down to disconnect him.

"No, *Dottore*, no! Please, no do this. It make things worse!"

He shook his head then went to an old, gray-painted, double-drawer filing cabinet and took out an envelope.

I was astonished when I saw him begin counting out twenty-dollar bills—ten of them. He gave the wad to the woman and held her hands.

"Maria, take this. Go away. Leave him. I don't want to see either you or your baby dead. Please ... for Ignatio."

She stood there silently for a moment staring at the floor then took the money and stuffed it into the top of her dress. She was crying as she picked up her son. Dr. Agnelli put his hand on her shoulder and walked her out, all the time telling her it would be all right.

I wasn't sure what to do. After what I had just witnessed, nothing I could say would be important. I turned to leave but stopped as the good doctor returned and sat in the old, spring-sprung desk chair. He put his hands to his face briefly then looked up at me. He seemed emotionally drained.

"Uh, I can come back another time, Dr. Agnelli."

"No, Berto, no. Sit down. You look excited. You got a girlfriend, young man?"

Jeez, did I have something tattooed on my forehead?

I blushed again.

"Sit down, Berto, sit down."

He went to the refrigerator and took out a Moxie, popped the cap off the bottle, and handed it to me. He picked up his cup of day-old cold coffee and sipped it. I never could drink that stuff. Still can't.

"What's the story?"

His eyes twinkled even through the fatigue. He looked at me and smiled.

"Berto, I'm a guy, too. Been there, done that. *Capice?*"

I blushed even more and kept looking at the floor.

"What's her name?"

"Bernice."

What he said next stunned me.

"Little Bernice Johnson?"

I couldn't help but grin.

"She's not so little anymore."

He burst out laughing.

"Neither are you, Berto. Neither are you. Now, how can I help you? I think we've already done the birds and bees bit, haven't we? Besides, if you get even close to that I will box your ears until they fall off. You hear me, young man?"

I gulped, "Yes, sir."

"So, what's your question?"

"Uh, what do girls like? You know ... what makes them happy?"

"Berto, you ask a question that has plagued us men ever since Eve fell in with that serpent and lured poor old Adam to his doom. What you're really asking is how could you make this girl like you, right?"

I nodded.

"You're lucky. Thirteen-year-old girls aren't too expensive to please. Later on, well, hold onto your wallet, kid. Things will get pretty costly."

Ah, Corrado, my old mentor, you don't know how right you were. I wish I had remembered your words of wisdom in medical school.

"Right now, Berto, the safest thing is to give her some sweets and maybe take her to the Saturday cartoon show at the theater. Then, if it seems right, stop at the parlor for an ice cream soda. How's that sound?"

It sounded great. Only problem was my name wasn't Rockefeller.

A smile creased his face, as he seemed to read my mind.

"Let's see, two movie tickets, two ice-cream sodas, some candy—oh, and a haircut, too, Topsy. Think two bucks will do it?"

He reached into that magic drawer once more and took out a pair of bills.

Strange. I still remember looking at those two pieces of gray-green currency with the blue seal and the words SILVER CERTIFICATE on them. I had never held so much money before.

I couldn't say anything. It was hard for me to keep my eyes from misting. He ran his hand through my unruly hair and shook my hand. We were now fellow members of the male brotherhood.

On to Thomas the Barber.

"Berto, you no come by a while. You have girl?"

Okay, I give up. Forget the blushing bit. I was ready to shout, "Yeah, I'm horny as hell about this girl."

What I did instead was grin and nod my head.

"She got big bazookas, kid?"

He cupped his hands on his chest to demonstrate then laughed as I did blush. Damn the autonomic nervous system!

In a weird way, embarrassing as hell as it was, I was proud that he was able to speak to me that way. Thirteen-year-old guys feel grown up if a real adult thinks they're old enough for some locker-room humor.

"What is girl's name?"

"Bernice."

"Chocolate girl I see hanging with you?"

I had never heard that expression before. I won't say what I had heard.

"She's beautiful, Thomas ... and smart, too."

Then he turned serious.

"Berto, you know I travel world, meet many, many girls."

He sighed.

"I wish I your age again."

Then he looked right at me.

"Color? Mean nothing, boy. It what here..." He tapped his forehead. "And here." He tapped his chest. "You old enough I tell about North African girl I meet 1921. Want hear?"

"Uh ... ummm ... not today, Thomas. I'm gonna ask Bernice to go out with me on Saturday."

Two days away. It seemed like forever.

He raised his hand in forbearance, walked to the back of the shop, opened the old chestnut-wood ice box, took out two Moxies, and handed me one. Good thing there was nothing wrong with my bladder then. Now? Well ... you know.

"Here, Berto, sit in chair."

He pointed to the one in the middle, and I hopped up on it—it had been years since I needed that booster cushion. He started to twirl the protective sheet around my neck, when in through the doorway strode Samuel Welch Sr. His son Sammy was my classmate, a mean sonofabitch, and his father was even meaner. He wore his police uniform like a license to harass and bully the locals. He knew he could get away with it, too. The folks here were all immigrants and feared what the police stood for. It was a shame. Most officers were there to help. Sam Sr. was the exception but, like the proverbial bad apple, he gave the rest of the force a black eye.

"Thomas, I'm in a hurry. I need a shave and a haircut now."

"I work on kid first."

"That damned dago? Get outta the chair, ya little wop."

I quickly vacated my seat. Welch gave me a canine-tooth smirk, and

I felt a shiver down my back.

Thomas said nothing. He wrapped the pinstripe sheet over the cop and started his routine. Snip-snip click, snip-snip click. He seemed to go faster and faster, his scissors in one hand and comb in the other, both hands moving like giant, gray-brown spiders over Welch's scalp. The hair flew off his head onto the floor. I got up and grabbed the old broom lying against the back wall. I swept the clippings into a dustpan and emptied them into the trash barrel.

Welch snickered as he watched me work.

"Yeah, kid, now yer learning a trade."

Thomas finished the haircut then began to lather the man's face. He didn't bother to strop the razor. As it slid across the stubbled cheeks I saw small rivulets of blood seeping down the cop's thick neck from behind and onto the back of his uniform.

Thomas finished and wiped Welch's face. As he stood up from the chair, he looked at me one more time.

"Hey, kid, you the one hangin' 'round with that...?"

What he said is not for family consumption.

"Your parents know? Hell, you organ grinders ain't got much taste, but it ain't natural what yer doin'."

I have to stop and catch my breath. Even now, many decades later, I wish I could go back in time and throttle that bastard.

If you're too young to know, things were different then. Harry Truman was leaving office, and the administration of former General Dwight David Eisenhower was about to begin. Civil rights leaders were still fighting mostly losing battles. It would be two years before the Supreme Court handed down *Brown v. Board of Education* and three years before a courageous lady named Rosa Parks kick-started the revolution on that bus in Birmingham, Alabama.

Samuel Welch Sr. was bigotry in the flesh. If he had lived in Birmingham he would have been one of Bull Connor's finest.

He got up, handed Thomas four bits (fifty cents to you youngsters) then tossed a nickel at me.

"Here, kid, go eat some pisgetti."

He guffawed, as I bent over and picked the coin off the floor, a buffalo nickel.

I let out my breath, as he strutted away unaware of the bloodstain on his shirt. The hair on the back of his head didn't look right, either.

Thomas put his finger to his lips, winked, and pointed to another barber chair.

"I no want you sit where scum sit. I must scrub chair with soap."

"I'll do it for you, Thomas."

That day, he gave me the best haircut I ever had. Then he rubbed the back of his hand over my front lip and cheeks.

"You man now, Berto. I give you shave."

By golly, so he did—my first shave. Wow!

I kept my word. I scrubbed that barber chair, and as I finished Thomas lightly punched my shoulder. He winked and laughingly told me to stop by early Saturday.

"I put cologne your face. Girls like nice smell."

I started to think it was gonna be one helluva Saturday!

I headed back home at a fast pace. As I passed Mr. Ruddy's shoe-repair shop, I felt the sole on my left shoe start to flop loosely. My feet were growing even faster than the rest of me, and these were the only shoes that fit even remotely. This I did not need. I hoped he was still open.

I peered through the window and, sure enough, I saw the cobbler sitting on his toadstool-shaped swivel chair. I had long since stopped being distracted by the absence of anything below his waist.

I walked in and apologized for bothering him so late in the day.

"Mr. Ruddy, the sole on my left shoe is starting to work loose, and I..."

"He's trying to say he's got a date on Saturday, Mr. R."

What the hell? It was Sal's voice but. . .

Then I looked up and there he was, hanging upside down from the ceiling bars and ropes that Mr. Ruddy used to move around the little workplace. He let himself drop to the floor, monkeylike, and put his hand on my shoulder.

"Old Berto here's got a girlfriend. I think he's in heat."

Harold Ruddy's brilliant blue eyes scanned me. He raised one humongous, muscled arm and held out his hand. I took off the shoe and handed it to him. Those huge fingers peeled off the remaining sole like it was paper. He examined that shoe, and then the one still on my right foot, and shook his head.

"Berto, your shoes need a good burial. Don't you have another pair?"

I was too embarrassed to answer, and Sal knew it. He looked at Mr. Ruddy and shook his head then patted my shoulder to comfort me.

I felt like crying. Everything had been going so well. How could I even go to school, much less a date, without shoes that fit?

Mr. Ruddy understood. He pointed to a shelf along the side wall. "Berto, see if any of those fit."

"Mr. Ruddy, I can't take someone else's shoes!"

"Kid, they've all been sitting there for months. The damned deadbeats who brought them never returned. They're mine now, and I think you two fellas are smart enough to realize I can't use them.

"Come to think of it, little Miss Sally, get yourself a pair, too. I've seen you sniffin' 'round that Cynthia girl. God, you two guys are turnin' inta ruttin' alley cats!"

That Yoda-like, legless, mushroom man laughed as Sal the big oaf blushed—first time I ever saw that. Mr. Ruddy was right. Sal's shoes were in about the same shape as mine.

We stumbled over each other to reach that shelf of dreams. Sal grabbed a set of oxfords and I reached for a pair of brown wingtips.

They fit!

Mr. Ruddy surveyed the two of us, as we sat on the floor and pulled on our own versions of Dorothy's ruby slippers.

"You guys have fun with your dates. God, I still remember that one mademoiselle from Gay Paree. Damned if she didn't give me the clap. Good thing that artillery shell cured it."

Sal and I knew what the clap was by then. We also knew about rubbers. The older kids kept them in their pockets to impress the younger guys like us.

"Have fun, but be careful. We don't need any little Sals and Bertos around here—least not yet. And Berto..."

He paused, uncertain about whether he should say more. Then he tipped his head and continued.

"Berto, your girl. She's really the bee's knees."

Sal and I exchanged looks.

"She's good lookin' and cute. Understand?"

We nodded.

"She's also ... different."

He speeded up his words before I could protest.

"Berto, listen. I'm different, too. Look at me. You know what I mean. You also know there are assholes out there who live to attack what they don't understand, what they fear out of ignorance."

I had never heard Mr. Ruddy talk like this. I thought of Samuel Welch Sr.

"Son, all I want is to warn you. Be careful."

We both stood up.

"Mr. Ruddy, can I stay and watch you awhile?"

"Sal, you want to be a shoemaker?"

Oh, Sal, I wish to God you had become a shoemaker. You might have lived a lot longer than you did.

"I dunno. What you do looks neat. 'Sides, bet I can beat you arm wrestling now, old man."

Sal had been working out with weights and was really getting strong.

Harold Ruddy's eyes lit up. He swirled around in his chair, put his giant-sized arm on the counter and said, "Come and get it, boy!"

I left as the two musclemen gripped hands.

Mama and Papa were sitting at their respective chairs at the table waiting for me to come home for dinner. Papa spotted my shoes first, and I immediately had to explain what happened—and that, no, I didn't owe Mr. Ruddy money I didn't have.

Mama showed me a shirt and a pair of pants she had been saving for me. She smiled and said they were special date pants. Papa winked at me!

It was Friday... one more day. The morning classes ended with the twelve o'clock bell, and we all raced out to the playground. It was warm enough to lean against the dark-red, brick-walled building. A relic of the nineteenth century, it still possessed gas lamps, in place but no longer used.

Angie, Tomas, Sal, and I ate the food we had brought wrapped in sheets of newspaper. Our families couldn't afford metal lunch boxes. Mama had given me an apple and a cabbage sandwich. We had just finished when we heard some of the girls screaming and yelling Sammy Welch's name.

I looked up to see the Welch kid pulling on Bernice's hair and calling her that hateful name. She was crying for him to stop.

I saw Sister Mercy Grace watching. She did nothing.

I ran over and yelled at him to quit it. He snickered and called me another name having to do with Bernice's ancestry, my affection for her, and my own ancestry. His face became feral, as he faced me and held up his arms, fists clenched.

Sam's father had taught him to box, and he knew he could put my lights out easily.

Tomas and Angie wanted to help, but Sal held them back. I heard him telling them that I had to do this myself.

I did the only thing a gentleman could do when faced with overwhelming odds. I yelled "Pearl Harbor" and kicked him in the balls.

Out of nowhere Sister Mercy Grace suddenly appeared next to me. She grabbed my left ear and started to pull me toward the principal's office. Once more I heard Sal.

This time it was a man's voice.

"Leggo his ear, Sister!"

She stopped on a dime, turned to look at him—and let go. Through clenched teeth she told me follow her. We walked through an honor guard of other kids, some of the girls blowing kisses to me. It would have been a real turn on if I hadn't known what my destination was.

I stood before Sister Dominic Grace. She was smaller than I was, but she was mighty, exuding an aura of authority none of us dared challenge. She was not only principal of the school but also Mother Superior of the adjacent convent. Except for the parish priest, she was the Big Boss.

"Roberto Galen, you surprise me. I've never had to discipline you before."

She turned to Sister Mercy Grace.

"What happened?"

I stood in open-mouthed amazement as this so-called woman of God made me the aggressor. She made no mention of Sammy's bullying of Bernice or his awful language. I couldn't help it. I turned to her and shouted, "That's not true!"

In for a penny, in for a pound, as they say.

I rattled off what happened and finished by asking Sister Dominic

Grace to call in Bernice and some of the other kids in to verify my story.

"Roberto, go on back outside. Go to the boy's room and wash your face and hands."

She opened the door to her office and let me out. As I walked away, I heard Sister Mercy Grace's voice rise as she snarled, "I warned you not to let that ... that girl come here."

I also heard Sister Dominic.

"Who are you to question my authority, Mercy Grace?"

I ran out into the cool air of the schoolyard, where I saw my friends waiting. Bernice was there. She came toward me, kissed me on the cheek, and whispered "thanks, white chocolate."

"See you at the movie house tomorrow?"

I looked at her, my fingers mentally crossed.

She grinned and nodded!

I will never forget that Saturday

True to his word, Thomas sprayed me with bay rum cologne. I could have been used as a Japanese beetle lure by the time he was done. I wore my "new" shoes and sported the "new" church-basement polo shirt and pants Mama had gotten me and lengthened to fit my growing legs.

We met in front of the Empire Theater and, for the first time, I had the price of admission. I plunked down one of those silver certificates and got two quarters back. Then we spent the next three hours watching Bugs Bunny being stalked by and outwitting Elmer Fudd, Daffy Duck doing his whacko stuff, and several Three Stooges shorts. I bought her popcorn, and we munched away, as Porky Pig stuttered himself into saying "That's all, folks!"

Afterwards we stopped by Bill's Burger Joint for two milkshakes—hers vanilla, mine chocolate. Then we walked.

Popcorn, milkshakes ... those only last so long in a teenager's body. That's when I steered Bernice toward that little candy shop. I opened the door to go in then realized she was still standing outside.

"Come on," I said. "Pick your poison, whatever you want."

I was feeling generous with other people's money.

"Uh, let me wait out here, Berto."

"Oh, okay."

I walked in and surveyed the selections in the candy counter. I put my hands on the glass even though the sign said DON'T TOUCH and peered at the dentist's delights within: chocolate kisses, Hershey bars, Mounds, a new square bar called Chunky, chewing gum, jelly beans ... and something weird. I had never seen them before: little bottles shaped like musical instruments, zoo animals, and just bottle shapes. Within them were strange red, green, yellow, and even blue liquids. They lay next to the big red wax lips, bubblegum cigars, and boxes of sugar-molded candy cigarettes.

I heard a rustle and looked up to see Mrs. Donnelly glaring at me from behind the counter. White hairdo, fair skin still showing the remnants of youthful freckling, and a protruding jaw I would learn to call prognathic in medical school. Her blue, near-sighted eyes peered at me over wire-rimmed glasses, as she croaked out, "What do you want, boy?" Her ill-fitting dentures clicked and clacked as she spoke.

I pointed at the Hershey Kisses.

"Gimme ten a' those, please."

As she reached for them, I asked for two of the new Chunky bars and two Hershey bars with almonds.

If that wasn't enough to set your teeth to aching, I also asked for a pack of the candy cigarettes and one wax lips. And then I pointed at those strangely fascinating little wax bottles.

"Ma'am, what are those?"

"They got sweet syrup in 'em, boy."

"Gimme one 'a each flavor, ma'am."

"You got enough money, kid?"

I held out the other dollar bill, and she snatched it out of my hand. A minute later she handed me a quarter, a nickel, and a dime, and a small, white, wax-paper bag filled with the goodies I had picked out.

I think she short-changed me, but there were no prices marked on the case, so I couldn't complain.

I walked to the door, opened it, and then had a second thought.

I called to Bernice, "Come on in, see if there's anything else you want. Look what I got you!"

She stuck her head in the door and suddenly I heard a yell bordering on a scream.

"Get outta my shop! We don't allow your kind in here."

I grabbed Bernice's hand and ran out. We walked about twenty feet, then I opened the bag and saw her eyes light up, as she saw the candy. I reached in, took out two chocolate kisses, removed the foil wrapping, and popped one in her mouth. I ate the other one. She laughed as some of the chocolate smeared my face.

"Berto, now you look like me!"

She kissed me on the cheek, and I tingled all over.

Back at the candy store, we heard the door open and then a familiar voice.

"See you later, Mama."

Sister Mercy Grace left the shop and headed back to the school. We ducked into a doorway, so she couldn't see us.

Monday morning I felt great as I hopped out of bed. For the first time I actually was looking forward to school. But when I got there a new nun had taken over our class—and I couldn't find Bernice.

Sister Mercy Grace had been transferred to a convent in Selma, Alabama.

Bernice Johnson, my beautiful wonderful Bernice, also had been transferred out to "restore a semblance of discipline" at the school.

Years later I saw her on TV, standing near Reverend Martin Luther King, Jr. Later still I read of a group of civil rights activists who had gone to Mississippi and suddenly disappeared. The newspaper article described the discovery of their mutilated bodies.

Damn you to hell, Sister No!

The Tin Man

They shall take up serpents; and if they drink any deadly thing, it shall not hurt them; they shall lay hands on the sick, and they shall recover. (Mark 16:18)

"Move it, Galen!"

The emergency-room resident darted like a flickering flame, as he went from one patient to the next and drove me to keep up. He only knew two speeds—flat out and dead stop—which was why he was pushing even though it was a quiet Thursday night. Twenty unfortunate souls awaited our healing touch.

"You're okay, kid. You just ate too much. Take him home, Mom."

The resident winked at the boy, as his mother gathered him and departed.

"Next!"

"It's not broken, just a bad sprain. Next time no hula-hoops. You're a bit long in the tooth for that."

I was the only one to hear his sub-vocalized "idiot," as the overweight, fiftysomething guy limped out.

"Next!"

We moved toward the patient-laden gurney, when the ER doors

burst open, and an ambulance driver and his helper wheeled in a stretcher at break-neck speed.

"Snake bites, multiple! Not good," the driver blurted out, as he slid the victim right under our noses.

The unit clerk, a female Cerberus guarding the gates of emergency health care, entered huffing and loudly hurling imprecations at the breach of etiquette … until she saw the guy lying ashen and gasping, his right hand and arm a swollen cerulean blue. I could see multiple sets of double-puncture wounds on the top and side of the guy's wrist. The poison's enzymes were already breaking down his skin, and the discoloration was marching up the forearm to the elbow. The venom did its number despite the makeshift, torn-shirt tourniquet.

The floor nurse and I began drawing blood and starting multiple IV sites. I heard the resident yell, "Cut-down tray! Looks like rattlesnake. Do we have any antivenin?"

It was a calculated risk. It is not unusual for snake venom to cause changes in blood clotting and lead to heavy bleeding.

He turned to me.

"Give him a dose of tetanus antitoxin and tetanus immune globulin. Piggyback two grams cephalothin in his left arm."

He turned to the nurse.

"I need a hundred milligrams solu-cortef four and point-five cc's epinephrine, subcu. Two milligrams morphine IM."

For all you medically savvy types, this episode happened long before you were born, so don't snicker and think that poor resident was a quack. At the time, what he ordered up was state of the art.

Snake bites are dirty. The poison can cause massive drops in blood pressure and the treatment itself can kill. It's also not unusual for someone to be allergic to the antivenin.

"Here, Galen, scrub his ventral (underside) forearm down with betadine and alcohol then glove up."

I did, and what I saw next I will never forget.

The resident took a scalpel with a number-ten blade and slit the snake handler's forearm from top to bottom. The venom-swollen skin peeled back like an invisible zipper.

Thank goodness the guy was not a bleeder, and thank God the morphine worked.

"Okay, Galen, we just did an emergency fasciotomy. It'll give his tissue breathing room."

Snake venom, especially rattlesnake venom, is powerful stuff. The snake has its own hypodermic needle fangs, and when it bites, the venom goes under the skin. Then chemicals in the venom start to digest and break down tissue. The more venom injected the more severe the effect.

The body responds by releasing immune-system chemicals that cause swelling. Like the proverbial two quarts of water in a one-quart container, pressure builds up and cuts off needed blood flow to the muscle tissue—so it dies.

By surgically splitting open the swollen limb, the resident gave the tissue room to expand, and blood flow resumed. Because of unintended consequences, it is not often recommended, but this time was an exception.

The pharmacy tech ran down the hall with an ice bucket. Our patient was in luck. The hospital had enough vials of rattlesnake antivenin on hand. That was not often the case. Back then it was scarce. But the James River had overflowed during heavy rains two weeks before, and the health service had requested a hefty supply in case the snake population decided to greet humans foolish enough to walk along the river bank.

"We need to do a quick skin test."

The resident carefully drew about a drop of the antivenin into a syringe normally used to give TB skin tests and went to the patient's opposite side. He slipped the tiny needle just under the skin, and the injected droplet formed a tiny mound on the man's upper arm.

Then we waited.

Skin testing is one of those medical roulette wheels. The gods decide—thumbs up or thumbs down. If the patient reacts to the tiny dose, life becomes more complicated for us—and him.

No reaction! Lord Shiva and Lady Kali had blessed the moment.

The resident injected the antivenin, and the nurse prepared the patient for transport to a monitoring unit. He moved on to the next case, and I turned to the ambulance driver.

"Rick, what's the story?"

I had noticed him standing in the corner watching us sweat and cuss … and hope. He was a young guy, probably a college student working part time for food money, and I saw the look in his eyes. I recognized the symptoms, because I have suffered from them my entire life: This one wanted to go to medical school.

Rick Shepland stretched his rangy frame.

"Whew, I didn't think he'd survive the ride! Never saw anything like that before."

It was strange. Here I was, talking to a guy just a few years my junior, and I could spot the fire in him, the overwhelming drive. I didn't have much time. I needed a minute to cool off, but I wanted to hear what the kid had to say.

"Uh … Dr. Galen … well, we got this call from a church out in southeast Richmond. Good people from what I could see, but they were a little strange. The place was filled with baskets. The baskets were filled with rattlesnakes and copperheads. Seems they take a passage from the Bible literally. They express their belief and faith in God by handling poisonous snakes."

I had read about snake worshippers—actually, snake handlers—people very strong in their faith, an offshoot of a group of believers in West Virginia.

"Well," Rick continued, "apparently the congregation had had two worship services. This guy is their assistant pastor. Part of the ritual involves reaching into one of the baskets, picking up a snake from behind its head, and holding it up and ... uh ... I guess, caressing it.

"The way the folks told it, the minister didn't have any trouble at first. He kept picking out snakes, even passing them to the other faithful, while the music and singing kept going. Then, when he put his hand in another basket, he suddenly let out a scream. They said he kept saying 'I believe, I believe,' then let out another scream and fell to the floor, tipping over the basket. At least four, maybe five, rattlers had sunk their fangs into his hand."

"How long before you got there?"

"That's the other strange thing. This happened hours ago. The head pastor and the flock just kept praying over the guy until he started to have trouble breathing. That's when we got called."

Rick shook his head. I think he wanted to cry. I understood. I put my hand on his shoulder.

"Great job, kid."

He smiled at me, nodded, and then mumbled, "Gotta go now, Doc. Thanks. See ya 'round."

I admit it. My student ego swelled a bit.

That evening I walked into the townhouse apartment I shared with Dave, aka Country Boy. He had gotten there just a few minutes before and was padding around the kitchen in socks and jock.

It was a bachelor pad, after all.

"Guess what I saw today!"

"Bet it doesn't beat my patient, City Boy."

He stuffed one of his awful concoctions of pickles and canned beans on two-week-old bread into his mouth and grinned, as I made pretend retching motions.

We both got out "snake bite case" simultaneously.

He was the student on call, when my ER patient reached the monitor unit.

We compared notes, and then he grinned.

"You ever been to a snake-worship service?"

He already knew the answer.

"Good, we're goin' this weekend. We're both off Sunday afternoon, right?"

"Yeah," I sighed.

Naturally, I wasn't enthusiastic. The last time he had shown me some of his down-home culture, we wound up at a Ku Klux Klan meeting.

Dave was no snake handler. He was a fallen-away Southern Baptist, and he harbored just enough devil in him to tease and torment a city kid like me. Too bad I never had the chance to take him on a tour of my old neighborhood. He would have been eaten alive.

Did I go? Yes.

It could have been a scene right out of the *National Geographic*. But instead of Javan natives in grass skirts, these dancers were southern whites in various, go-to-Sunday-meeting clothes. Guitars, violins, and at least a half-dozen young women singing added to the cacophony of the head preacher and his acolytes speaking in tongues while doing a good imitation of whirling dervishes.

As the fervor peaked the preacher and other members of the congregation reached into several wicker baskets and pulled out good-sized pit vipers. They continued their tarantella-like dance, while kissing the snakes and waving them about. Some even wrapped them around their necks.

Dave and I stood as far to the rear as possible. Even then we had to duck to avoid having a reptile shoved in our faces.

We left early.

"How'd ya like it, City Boy?"

I had to clear my throat to avoid squeaking out a reply. I managed to say "pretty tame stuff."

Dave poked me in the gut and laughed.

"Bullshit!"

That night I hit the sack around midnight, after stuffing my head with textbook chapters and journal articles. Non-phallic images of snakes whirled around me, and my mind returned to the past.

Berto's young world had its share of ministers and tent revival meetings ... and snakes.

"Berto, take a look at this."

Dr. Agnelli had his new-fangled, wood-cased electrocardiogram machine hooked up to a man maybe in his late forties. The guy didn't seem to be in any distress.

"See?"

My mentor had taught me some of the basics—how to name the little squiggles on the paper and what they meant. I had learned to recognize normal heart beats, but I had not seen these before.

"You mean those big, tooth-shaped waves?"

"Yes. That means the reverend here is putting out some extra beats. They're called premature ventricular contractions."

"You mean the big chambers of his heart are beating funny?"

Score one for the kid.

He patted me on the head.

"Good boy, Berto. You got it. Now, what else can you tell me?"

My ego swelled that day, too.

"Uh ... there's only a few and they only happen every ten or so beats."

Not bad for a tenement kid.

"Let's talk with our patient after he gets dressed."

The doctor and I sat in the small anteroom and waited for the man to put his shirt on. He was average height, about five-feet, ten inches, and a little stocky at one-hundred-ninety pounds. Laugh-line creases with some remnants of past grief webbed outward from his dark-brown eyes and toward the thick sideburns hanging down from his shag hair-cut. He wore a vest and a jacket that didn't match his pants.

"Berto, this is the Reverend Donald Halloway. He's visiting our little paradise and wants to save our souls."

I saw Corrado Agnelli's eyes sparkle with mixed sarcasm and devil-may-care, don't-give-a-damn laughter. It wasn't until I left for medical school that I understood my mentor's cynicism about the clergy. By then he knew he was dying.

"I don't feel right, Doc," Halloway began. "I was in the middle of my sermon about the wiles of the Devil, and how we needed to cast the Foul Serpent from our souls, when my heart started to skip. I felt dizzy. I couldn't breathe. I had to stop."

Reverend Halloway had one of those not-quite-tenor voices that could really do justice to the word "Gawd." Despite that I could see that Dr. Agnelli considered the man sincere in his beliefs and genuinely wanting to help people.

"Reverend, sometimes the heart gives out an extra beat, kinda like an extra drumbeat. That's what shows on the paper here. It doesn't look like a bad situation, but knowing how hard you work, I think you should see a good cardiologist, someone who specializes in these things."

Remember, this was back in the day when specialists and sub-specialists were rare creatures. So I could tell that Dr. Agnelli was concerned, even though the reverend's heart tracings didn't appear so bad. I learned it was the sign of a really good doctor: the gut feeling that the test wasn't telling the whole story.

Dr. Agnelli scribbled a phone number on his prescription pad and handed it to the preacher. Halloway took it and thanked him. Then he stared at me, those dark-brown eyes mounted by thick eyebrows trying to fathom my role in life.

"Boy, have you accepted the Lord Jesus Christ as your Savior?"

Agnelli cleared his throat and carefully enunciated: "His name is Berto, Reverend."

"Uh ... yes, of course, doctor. Berto, my boy, do you believe in God?"

My mentor was standing behind him and nodding his head in a big yes.

I took the hint and replied accordingly.

"Good. Come by this afternoon. We're having a call to the Lord at four o'clock."

He mentioned a vacant lot near the business district.

"Make sure you call the heart doctor, Reverend."

The preacher left, and Dr. Agnelli immediately sat down. He looked at me questioningly.

"You think I was too hard on him, Berto?"

At my young age subtlety and political correctness were not part of my nature—still aren't.

"Uh ... I think you think he has a problem, and I don't think you like what he does."

"Ah, you don't disappoint me, Berto. No, I'm sure the Reverend Halloway is a good man, an honest man. It's just that I've seen some bad stuff done in the Lord's name. I have a hard time separating the wheat from the chaff, so to speak."

"Is he really sick?"

"Yes, but there's not much I can do for him. If he were having chest pain I could give him nitroglycerin tablets. But this ... this is a problem in how his heart beats. Maybe someday there'll be some magic pills we can use. But now, well, I'll be surprised if even a heart specialist can offer him anything but nerve medication."

Corrado, my friend, if you were alive today you would be amazed.

That Sunday afternoon was all anyone could ask for: warm, mid-spring breezes, bright sun in a cloudless sky. I had snatched a quick lunch at home then ran out again to find my friends. But Tomas and Angie were nowhere to be seen. Sal sat on the stoop of his building, and I could tell that his father had just given him a beating.

"Hey, Berto," he said, weakly.

I didn't make an issue about it. It wouldn't help. His old man was a mean drunk. It wasn't until the demon hormones of puberty took hold of Sal that he got even. For now, he suffered and kept that big sloppy grin on his face.

"Come on, Sal, let's go save your soul!"

"I ain't got one, you big turd! Don't you remember? The nuns all say I ain't worth savin'."

"See, that proves you need to be saved. Let's go listen to the Reverend Halloway. 'Sides, it's free!"

That did it.

He laughed, and we jackknifed down the street hurling insults at each other.

The big canvas tent filled the lot, where an old office building had burned down years before. Sometimes we would play baseball there, if the rats weren't too active. We approached the tent opening, and the man at the gate told us to go away, but I said Reverend Halloway had invited us. He looked at me, unsure of what to do, when I saw the preacher inside and yelled, "Hello Reverend!"

He turned to us.

"Oh, hello, Berto," he replied, smiling.

That convinced the guy at the entrance, and we went inside.

"I see you brought a friend."

He looked at Sal, and Sal grinned back. Then someone called him away, so we grabbed seats as far back as we could.

The tent filled quickly, and while we all waited, a three-woman choir sang "Amazing Grace" in amazingly ungracious, off-key voices. An acolyte took the podium and enumerated the various encomiums the reverend had earned and then, religious barker that he was, proudly introduced the Reverend Donald Halloway to the sounds of trumpets, tambourines, and "hallelujahs" from choir and audience alike.

Sal belched, and I suppressed a giggle.

I have to admit, the Reverend could talk—and talk and talk. We knew it was drawing to a close, when his assistants picked up the offering baskets. Sal and I made a move to escape.

"And that, my brothers and sisters in the Lord, is why you should give yourself—give till it hurts."

Sal clutched his side pocket, mouthed "No way," and got up to leave.

"So remember my words, brothers and sisters. Follow the true way."

Then I heard him begin that signature phrase, the one he would become famous for:

"The Lord will…"

But he never completed it, because Sal had reached the tent exit and jumped with a start, yelling "SNAKE!"

Sal didn't like snakes.

Apparently, neither did the congregation. We barely got away before the crowd erupted behind us like ants after spilt food. The place emptied like a burst dam.

On my way out, I managed to catch a glimpse of the terror-inspiring reptile. It was a fat, black rat snake. Probably lived happily off the resident vermin. It beat a hasty retreat, too.

A few weeks later, I was hanging around the clinic as usual. I had polished off a bottle of Moxie and the sugar/caffeine contentment had set in. My curiosity, however, was unabated.

"Dr Agnelli, whatever happened to the reverend?"

He looked at me then surprised me with a question of his own.

"Did Salvatore do that on purpose?"

"Do what, sir?"

"You know darned well, young man. Yelling 'snake' inside that tent. Wish I had been there!"

He laughed but stopped when he saw me staring at him.

"Ah, yes, the Reverend Halloway. Seems that the loss of expected proceeds from that revival meeting forced him to move on. Not enough money here."

"Yes, sir. But what about his heart?"

"I don't know. He never went to see the cardiologist."

Dr. Agnelli grabbed another bottle of Moxie, tossed it to me, and sat down next to his cold coffee. He winked and asked, "Berto, what have you learned from this?"

My eleven-year-old voice did its best to imitate that unforgettable tenor.

"The Lord will provide, if your wallets don't hide."

He sipped his cold coffee, and I guzzled down the Moxie.

When a man's an empty kettle
He should be on his mettle
And yet I'm torn apart.
Just because I'm presumin'
That I could be kind of human
If I only had a heart.
—E.Y. "Yip" Harburg

The Nazi

He who looks down his nose at others sees only his own crotch.
—*Mark Levin*

I hate May.

Yes, I know, the trees are leafed out, the flowers are blooming, the grass is greening up, and the birds are singing their little heads off.

But May also casts its cowl of grief and misery over my memory. The final month of medical school brought me an inverse Christmas gift list. I lost my fiancée, was nearly dismissed by the dean, and almost contracted syphilis.

"Galen, take that patient in 510. Work him up, and get me the blood. I gotta present him at residents' rounds tomorrow, so make it snappy."

I didn't like the intern. He was unnecessarily obnoxious and enjoyed riding the backs of the students under his supervision. He was also incompetent and used our conclusions as if they were his own.

Not that I bear grudges, but I must admit, years later when I learned that his license to practice medicine was yanked for *shtupping* too many of his female patients, I felt a certain sense of satisfaction.

So, there I was, approaching my new patient. It was quite a sight. He was tied down to his bed with restraints on all four limbs. Despite that, he had managed to toss and turn enough to cast off all bed coverings. He lay there, glory naked, yelling at the top of his lungs.

What crossed my mind at that moment? The same words found on "black-box" recorders recovered from crashed airplanes, the voices of the doomed pilots memorializing their final moments.

Okay, Galen. Go for it, kid.

I stood next to the metal, crank-up hospital bed—and just missed getting spat on, as more profanity spewed from his gray-stubbled, unshaved face. He looked about seventy but, as I saw from the date of birth on his entry sheet, he was only in his mid-forties.

I mentally composed the report I would write:

Forty-five-year-old Caucasian male, disoriented X 3, cachectic with protuberant ascitic abdomen and pronounced widespread spider veins. Peripheral wasting with yellow sclerae. Fetor hepatis of the breath, dry fissured tongue...

The magic doctor terms, drilled into me by four years of training, were this man's living epitaph. He had severe alcohol damage to the liver, wasting of the muscles in his arms and legs, and a belly distended by ascites fluid brought on by collapsing cell failure.

He was dying of self-induced liver disease.

Still, that didn't explain the wild-eyed stare and distorted grin or those demon-yellow, jaundiced eyes following my every move. No, this wasn't the wild delirium of metabolic compromise or the apathetic quiet of the usual terminal cirrhotic patient.

Once more I escape a dousing, this time as his bladder emptied in a weak stream of brown urine. I placed a small, rubber tourniquet hose around his left arm, felt for an almost-non-existent vein, and found it. I took the glass syringe from the tray I carried, wiped the skin over the vein with an alcohol-saturated cotton ball, and stuck the needle in.

Ah, blood!

Only those who must daily take samples from humans whose vessels have preceded the rest of their body to the grave can understand the satisfaction of seeing a successful, blood-drawing stick.

I pulled back on the plunger, and trickles of dark-red liquid oozed into the syringe barrel. Piece of cake.

Just then the bed shook, and I heard the impossible before I saw it. That wasted patient's right arm managed to snap its restraint. Before I knew it, a cadaverous hand had reached over, grabbed the syringe out of its partner left arm and, as blood erupted from the venipuncture site, stabbed me in the neck.

I yelled a "goddammit," grabbed the syringe from the patient's hand, and quickly set it down on the table. My man was dribbling from his lips and laughing, while I attempted simultaneously to put a patch on his arm and press the throbbing puncture wound on my neck.

I quickly emptied the syringe into several tubes then almost ran back to the nursing station to get the samples out. I also had to report the needle stick.

Even in those benighted days, before vacutainer tubes, HIV, and hepatitis C infections, it was still de rigueur to report needle-stick accidents. The dangers back then included a mysterious illness caused by something called Australia antigen—later renamed Hepatitis B—and above all the specter of syphilis.

That was my greatest fear. My patient's behavior was more typical of syphilitic paresis or brain damage. Today's medical personnel fear HIV infection, but that is only an echo of the threat syphilis posed in my student days. The only good thing was it could be treated.

I marked the test down along with the metabolic workup for delirium and went to the head nurse to submit the accident report. What happened next was a revelation.

She burst out laughing.

Okay, I admit I wasn't the easiest person to get along with. My nickname, even among my best friends—my A-Team—was the Bear. The nursing staff respected my abilities as a student. They also knew that my girlfriend and fellow medical student, June, had dumped me the week before and—as women are wont to do—blamed me for not being more attentive to her. How could they know my inattentiveness was due to fatigue from working double shifts to buy June a ring?

I stared at the nurse until she stopped. She surveyed me once more then yelled, "Get the chief resident."

To her credit, she gave one of the blood tubes to another nurse and asked her to hand-carry it to the lab for a syphilis blood test—stat!

I headed for the doctors' lounge behind the nursing station and slumped into a chair. I was emotionally drained, so much so that I must have dozed off, because I suddenly felt myself being shaken and looked up to see the chief resident standing over me.

"Mr. Galen, I understand you got a needle stick. Show me."

I pulled down the side of my white tunic, and the resident repeated my earlier, aircraft-disaster-related words.

The room had no mirror, so I couldn't see the jagged puncture wound with secondary, fresh bruising spreading down the left side of my neck.

"You ordered a syphilis test?"

I nodded.

The head nurse entered the room carrying a suspicious-looking, covered tray. She whispered in the chief's ear, and he grinned and nodded.

"Mr. Galen, stand up."

I stood up.

"Your patient tested positive for syphilis. You know what that means don't you?"

I sat down again.

Yes, I knew what it meant, and now I knew what was in the devil tray.

Even today, one of the primary treatments for confirmed syphilis is a hefty dose of penicillin given through a Baltimore Harbor Tunnel-sized needle deep into the rump.

Other available treatments are less onerous, but back in the year of my graduation penicillin in large doses was primo. If you were allergic to penicillin, you were forced to take equally large, oral doses of erythromycin guaranteed to cause nausea, vomiting, and diarrhea.

"Mr. Galen, I said stand up!"

One did not disobey one's chief resident. I stood up again, sweat starting to form between my shoulder blades and slowly trickle down my back.

"Drop trou', Mr. Galen."

His wish was my command. I unbuckled my belt, unbuttoned my white trousers, and let them fall to the floor.

"Shorts down, too."

Boxers or briefs? Like a certain future president, I wore "tidy whities," and they, too, dropped down around my ankles. I stood there, my legs spread apart, hands on the window ledge to steady myself for what was coming next.

I was facing away from the lounge door. I had seen the resident close it and, since we were both guys and doctors, it wasn't too embarrassing. I heard the lid of the metal tray come off. I felt the coolness of the alcohol-saturated cotton ball rubbed over my right buttock.

There I was, bare bottom facing that hell-portal door, genitals swaying in the breeze of the air circulator, a shrunken pendulum responding to the fear-induced sympathetic nervous system.

The chief resident barked, in what I thought was an unnecessarily loud voice, "Hold on, Galen!"

The door flew open just as that stainless-steel fire hose with a barb on the end penetrated my flesh. I tried to turn as the resident pressed on the plunger, and the glue-like white goo spread through my gluteal muscle like liquid fire.

"Hubba hubba! Way to go..." and other assorted, lewd comments emanated from the entire nursing staff crowding the doorway.

I involuntarily jerked and said "unhh," as the resident pulled out the needle. A few faint gasps and "hmmms" from the audience punctuated the motion. I took a deep breath and felt the flush rising up my neck to my face.

"Okay, Galen, once more and we're done."

I shivered as that cold alcohol wipe slid across my left rump. The crowd in the doorway began to chant, "Stick it in, stick it in!"

Once more the fiery serpent spread, and this time my left gluteal went up in flames. Then with a yank the needle was out, and it was over. I pulled up my briefs to the accompaniment of whistles and "no, no, take it off, take it off!"

Damned perverts!

I pulled up my pants, zipped them, and turned around. Eleven pairs of hands clapped. Okay, I could play the game.

"Ladies and gentlemen, the next show will be in one hour."

I bowed, and they clapped louder.

As I exited the lounge, a rather pretty young nurse winked at me and whispered, "Wow, eight inches!"

I blushed again.

A male nurse, a retired army medic, also winked. I ignored him.

I walked down the corridor, whatever dignity I once possessed now gone. I tried to exorcise the pain from my bottom. It didn't work. I felt something wet running down the back of my legs and reached back— both hands were stained with blood. As I did so, a nurse came running up to me with a handful of paper towels.

"Mr. Galen, you're bleeding!"

I grabbed the towels and ran to the bathroom. I wasn't going to do another striptease in the hallway.

Those large-bore needle punctures were perfect conduits for blood.

The entire bottom of my trousers was stained with it. I stuck the paper towels in my underwear and went out to find the intern.

"May I have permission to go and change into scrubs or get another pair of whites?"

The bastard looked at my bloodstained trousers, then at me, and said, "No."

I worked the rest of the day enduring snide comments and questions about whether my cycle was early. One of my less-likeable classmates tried to get a rise out of me.

"Hey, Galen, if you're going to get syphilis at least have some fun."

I turned to the schmuck and flashed my best, angry-bear grin.

He backed up a step.

"Thanks, Murray, very thoughtful of you. Guess you don't have to worry about things like that. I understand that sheep and goats don't carry syph."

That evening at the apartment I shared the day with my roommate, Dave. I guess I groused and stomped so much he grew weary of it, because he got up and put his hand over my mouth.

"Get outta those rags and take a shower, City Boy. You'll feel better. Besides, you stink."

He was right. Blood does exude a unique odor as it ages.

I lay on my bed, muscles loosened by the wondrous healing powers of running hot water. I was in fresh pajamas, and my Cecil's "Textbook of Medicine" was open to the chapter on syphilis. I already knew most of what was in there, having read from Dr. Agnelli's textbooks and seeing him treat patients at the clinic.

I fell asleep, book on my chest.

I dreamed of Titus Londell.

In every neighborhood, rich or poor, mansions or tenements, there is always the oddball who stands well apart from the rest in how he thinks, speaks, acts, or behaves.

Titus Londell belonged exclusively to our little luxury enclave of soot and dirt.

Tom Seidlitz's mother had gone crazy with grief over the loss of her son in the Great War. Titus Londell was just ... well... crazy.

The Korean War had unofficially ended at Panmunjom in stalemate. President Truman had left the White House to President Eisenhower. And I was finishing eighth grade and looking forward to attending Concepción High School.

It also was the last year the four of us—Angie, Tomas, Sal, and I— would be in the same class. We sat in the little soda shop and ordered something new—Vanilla Coke—though none of us would have been there if Dr. Agnelli hadn't given me a buck as his way of celebrating my acceptance to that special high school. I think he would have come with us, if someone else could have spelled him at the busy free clinic.

I hated to admit it to the guys but, even after going out with other girls, I still missed Bernice. The only one I shared my feelings with was Sal and, muscle-bound ape that he was, he understood. He was becoming more and more a surrogate for the brother I never had.

We finished our soda pop and headed down the street along the river. As we passed Mr. Ruddy's, we heard a rapping on the window that made us stop and veer into his shoe-repair shop.

The last two Old Guys were sitting there, as usual polishing off some Rheingolds. Mr. Huff had never been the same since Mr. Brown died, but he always came by Mr. Ruddy's place. It was his substitute for church, I guess.

What surprised me was the third person in the room, doing a good job of keeping up with the other two in downing beers: Thomas the Barber.

Thomas Putchenkov was almost seventy-eight then, old enough to be the father of the Old Guys. He didn't look it, and he certainly didn't act like it either—he behaved like the youngest one in the room.

"Hello, Berto! Congrats!"

Mr. Ruddy's brilliant blue eyes flashed above his smile. I never ceased to be amazed at what he would say. For a man who left for war at age eighteen and came back a legless torso, his depth of understanding and knowledge on just about anything, from philosophy to history to girls, was encyclopedic.

Now, how did he know about Concepción?

"Why didn't you slackers make it like Berto?"

Mr. Huff looked at Sal, Tomas, and Angie and, for the first time that I could recall, he smiled.

"Aww ... we just didn't brown-nose the teachers like ol' Berto here. Hell, he probably dated every nun in the convent just to get good grades."

Sal stuck his tongue out at me and flashed that lopsided, shit-eating grin that was his trademark.

I miss you, Sal.

Angie joined the chorus.

"Yeah, didn't I see you kissin' ol' prune-face Sister Dominic last week? Didn't think we saw ya, did ya?"

Angie pursed his lips and smacked them in an exaggerated kiss.

Tomas nodded.

"Yeah, good thing they shipped out old Mercy Grace. She'd probably want ya ta cop a feel."

The whole room rocked with laughter—even from me.

Thomas belched and offered me a swig of his Rheingold. I admit I was tempted, but Mr. Ruddy put a stop to it.

"Come on, you old Bolshevik, it was your idea. Go get it."

"Me not Bolshevik. Maybe Menshevik, maybe even anarchist, but no matter. Here, Berto."

He went to Mr. Ruddy's little refrigerator, probably the only other one in the neighborhood besides the one in Dr. Agnelli's clinic, and took out ... a cold Moxie! He handed it to me after flipping off the cap on the opener screwed to the wall.

Sal just gawked.

"Don't we get any?"

Mr. Huff moved his head from side to side in a broad no, then he smiled and got out three more. Ten minutes later we four school chums were belching in time with the barber and the Old Guys, when Sal pointed out the window at the building across the street.

"Hey, looka that! Crazy Titus is at it again!"

It was weird. Picture a disjointed marionette of a man marching up and down in a goose-step that would have done old Adolph's brown shirts proud. Every other step his right arm would jerk up in that hated, *Sieg Heil* salute that had thrown much of the world into hellish chaos only a decade before.

It was pathetic—sad, actually—and in its own perverse way funny.

Remember the Three Stooges? They did a wonderful takeoff of the Axis leaders goose-stepping, each kicking the butt of the one in front, while singing a comedic takeoff song. I can still hear it:

"When Der Fuhrer says, 'Ve ist der master race,' ve heil! heil! right in Der Fuhrer's face."

Or was that a Spike Jones song?

Damned memory!

That was Titus Londell.

Harold Ruddy stared at the scene, and for a moment I thought he was going to cry.

"Mr. Ruddy, why is he like that?"

Both he and Mr. Huff got that faraway look ... the same one that appeared on both men when they talked about Tom Seidlitz.

"He was the fifth guy," Mr. Huff whispered.

Mr. Ruddy nodded.

"It was Tommy, me, George, Tim, and Titus. Four of us came back ... or maybe I should say three and a half."

He looked down at what was no longer there.

Mr. Huff took up the story.

"Harry and Tim were in the hospital for a long time. I wasn't right, either ... still ain't ... but I could work. Tim's lungs were shot to hell from that damned gas. It seemed like only Titus had come back in one piece.

"Now, you four young fellas gotta understand and maybe learn from our mistakes."

He turned to Putchenkov.

"Hey, Poochy, you did your share of sewing some wild oats, didn't you?"

Thomas also got that faraway look.

"You, betcha! I got more oats out there than lot of you!"

He grinned at me.

"Berto, I tell you story of girl in Africa?"

Many times since I had hit puberty, but I just nodded.

"You guys want I tell on others?"

Four kids and two Old Guys shook their heads emphatically.

"Hokay, but you no know what you miss."

He popped the top off another Rheingold and swigged it down then pitched the empty bottle into the big garbage can resting alongside the shoe-grinding equipment.

Mr. Ruddy took up the line again.

"Titus was the luckiest guy around. He came back ... no wounds, no crazy dreams ... and his girl actually waited for him."

Mr. Huff nodded.

"Well, old Titus, he ups and marries his gal, opens up a new-fangled thing called a gas station, and seemed to be sitting pretty. For fifteen years, even through the Depression, everything he touched turned to gold. Then ... well ... as the saying goes, the poop hit the fan."

Mr. Huff took over again.

"His wife noticed it first. He just wasn't quite right in ... uh ... bed, if you get my drift. Then he started to forget things and would laugh for no reason at all. He didn't remember things well.

"He was the smartest of us. Kinda reminds me of you, Berto," he said—just what I needed to hear.

Mr. Ruddy played tag-team again.

"See, guys, we weren't the quietest Yanks over in France. Hell, we voolay-vooed every skirt we could. I told you a while back that I caught the clap, and the only thing that cured me was that damned artillery shell. I don't recommend the treatment but, as you can see, I don't have the clap now."

Putchenkov interjected.

"Clap, that all? I ever tell you about girl with big teeth and big bazookas?"

"Yes!" came the unanimous vote.

"Hokay, I no tell you, but Thomas hurt long time after..."

He laughed then grew pensive, as Mr. Ruddy continued.

"Titus was just as wild as the rest of us, maybe more so. Intelligence has no monopoly on common sense. Understand, Berto?"

I gulped and nodded.

"Anyway, Londell's wife took him from doctor to doctor, and finally one sharp guy figured it out. Poor old Titus had contracted syphilis in '18, and it took fifteen years to start rotting his brain. There was no penicillin back then, and the treatments they used were no better than shaking a rattle while dancing around a fire."

My next comment only guys will understand. You know what happens when you jump into a cold swimming pool? Right. Things shrivel up and disappear. I think the four of us experienced that sensation, after Harold Ruddy finished speaking. I know I did.

We all turned to stare out at the contorted little man performing his grotesque dance across the street. Then Angie let out an "oh shit!" even though no crashing aircraft was in the vicinity.

Another unanimous sentiment.

Samuel Welch Sr., the corrupt police officer and a true pig by anyone's definition—including those of his hardworking, honest fellow officers—was doing his peacock strut down the street. He swung his heavy wooden billy club by its leather cord, and it was fairly obvious what was about to take place.

It seemed to happen in slow motion. Welch walked up behind Titus and swung that damned club as hard as he could against the back of the man's knees. Titus fell to the ground and began crying like an injured dog. Welch then proceeded to club him about the shoulders and chest. I noted that he carefully avoided hitting his victim's face.

I couldn't believe how fast Mr. Ruddy grabbed two, ski-pole-like sticks and began propelling his swivel chair out the door. Mr. Huff and Thomas ran after him.

The four of us brought up the rear.

Harold Ruddy seemed to glide across the street, heedless of the traffic. Those massive arms holding those sticks reminded me of some strange mushroom creature skiing down a slope. He reached Titus just as Welch was about to hit him in the groin. He jammed one pole into Welch's gut. As the bastard started to fall, Thomas came up behind him and with his own massive arms lifted the cop off the ground.

Welch tried to draw his gun, but Mr. Huff snatched it from his right hand, flipped the cylinder open, and emptied the bullets onto the ground. Welch was braying at the top of his lungs about assaulting a police officer and that we were all under arrest and would spend the rest of our lives in jail.

Mr. Ruddy nodded, and Thomas put the red-faced cop down but retained hold of his arms. The shoemaker pushed his swivel chair right up to Welch and reached forward with his left hand. He grabbed the cop's shirt and pulled him down to eye level.

"Welch, I know you. I knew your daddy, too. He was over there with us and, in case you're interested, he was the biggest coward I've ever seen. Tommy Seidlitz had to save his neck so many times because he tried to run. You ... you're a chip off the old block, ain't you? Seems to me you even weaseled your way out of serving in '41, didn't you? You goddamned chicken hawk!"

Mr. Huff bent over and picked up Titus, and as he held him in his arms, the little man bawled like a child.

Mr. Ruddy glared at Welch, who threatened to arrest us all once more.

"Listen up, boy. Chief Conmer was our sarge back then. He even called your father a piss-faced coward. So, George and I are going to have a little talk with him about you."

With that, he motioned for Sal to hand him the cop's billy club. He took it and held in front of Welch's face.

"If you ever touch Titus again—or anyone else around here, for that matter—you're gonna look like this."

Those two elephant leg arms held up the club, and my pals and I gasped as it snapped in two like a matchstick.

Putchenkov let Welch loose, and he ran down the street. George picked up the gun.

"Whadda we gonna do with this?"

"We'll return it to the chief. After all, we're good citizens."

Thomas took the whimpering Titus in his arms and carried him across the street, while Mr. Huff pushed Mr. Ruddy and his chair. We stayed behind and just stared at one another.

Angie broke the silence.

"I can't believe what just happened."

But it was true—the broken billy club lay on the ground as silent testimony to an amazing event.

Shortly afterward Samuel Welch Sr. was let go from the police force. No surprise, he joined the local mob as an enforcer. I would not realize the long-term consequences of that action until years later.

Need I say another story?

Titus Londell died in a mental institution my third year of medical school.

Strange, he outlived all my friends.

What could God have had in mind with that latter-day Job's suffering?

The Jew

I died one Saturday afternoon.

You read it right. I really did die. I was deader than Marley's ghost.

It was one of those rare weekends. I was totally caught up with my med-school assignments, springtime was in full bloom in Richmond, and the sun's warmth added to the torpidity of the tobacco-scented, breezeless air.

My roommate, Dave, was off wooing his *inamorata*, Connie, aka the Teacher, and good ol' Country Boy was in heat more often than an unneutered tomcat. He was taking full advantage of the fact that Connie's two apartment mates, Peggy and my girlfriend June, had gone to Virginia Beach until Sunday evening.

I, on the other hand, had been left in the lurch, when June, aka the Model, decided to accompany Peggy.

It's a good thing June and I shared a relationship that didn't involve shenanigans such as those engaged in by Connie and Dave. Yeah, right.

So there I sat, dorm door wide open, in my boxers and pretending to read a pathology book, when the kid next door knocked on the blond-stained, open portal.

"Hey, Galen, wanna help me out?"

Pat Tilden stood there, his face a vision of innocence. Slender, not quite five-feet, eight-inches tall and still not shaving, he was the third generation of his family to attend dental school. Fairly sharp-witted for a dental student, too.

Note: This is an inside joke among medical, dental, and graduate students. By definition medical students are academic drudges, while dental students are a bit more carefree—maybe because of the anesthetic gases they use. As for graduate students, well, enough said.

"I can't lend you any money. I don't have any."

I held up an empty wallet.

"I know. Everyone in the building knows. What I need is someone to practice on."

The hairs on the back of my neck started to rise. The last time I heard that expression, it was Dave wanting to practice DREs. We were studying the urogenital tract—kidneys, bladder, prostate, and reproductive organs—and we were supposed to use each other as guinea pigs. In med school the cheapest lab animals available are students. Even the professors used and abused us.

Digital rectal exams. I did get even, though.

Another story but maybe best left untold.

I felt relatively secure with Tilden. After all, what harm could a dental student do? He waited while I slipped on pants, tee shirt, and shoes, then he escorted me to the dental building several blocks away. I reveled in the unseasonably warm air, though I would have felt better if June hadn't been out of town.

We entered the granite-faced building that was, at the time, the newest on campus. I heard strange, and unsettling, whirring noises coming from a room—of course, that's where we were headed.

The space was large and open, with rows of tilt-back armchairs. It looked surreal, as though I had entered the largest barbershop in the world. The chairs were half-filled with patients draped and lying in various recumbent positions, while dental students shoved assorted devices in their mouths. I was about to crack a joke about that, when Tilden took my arm and led me to an open chair.

"Sit here, Galen, I'll be right back. I need to get a professor."

I should have left then.

Tilden returned shortly, now wearing a white smock, and following a gray-haired, blue-eyed, old man in knee-length lab coat. The man turned to Tilden, one eyebrow raised, and said, "Are you sure you want to work on him?"

He reached forward, grabbed my chin, pulled it down, and shined a flashlight inside my mouth. As he came near, I could smell a mixture of alcohol and tobacco on the breath emanating from his stubbled face. He really needed a shave and some strong mouthwash.

"Mr. Tilden, look at those molars!"

Pat had to stand on his toes to peer into my oral cavity.

"Jeez, what a mouthful!"

Professor Sommerfield, per his name tag, nodded.

"What's your name, boy?"

"Robert Galen, sir."

Tilden interjected. "He's a second-year medical student."

"Mr. Galen, your wisdom teeth are a disgrace. They need to come out."

Wisdom teeth? What an oxymoron. If I had been wise I would have thanked them for their attention and refused their offer. Instead I reached up and felt the inside of my mouth. Yes, my hind molars, upper and lower, were starting to jut sideways into my cheeks.

"Mr. Tilden, let's numb up this young man and get started."

Pat looked at me, guilt written all over his face.

"Uh ... Galen ... what we're gonna do is put some numbing medicine in your gums so nothing will hurt. Then we'll just pop out those bad old molars. Okay?"

"You're sure this isn't gonna hurt?"

"Naw, we do this all the time."

The professor returned with a covered, stainless-steel tray. He set it on the chair's side shelf and examined my mouth once more. The alcohol on his breath had been replenished.

"Mr. Tilden, where are you going to inject?"

Pat spouted certain anatomical locations in the mouth. I was familiar with them—but only from books and gross-anatomy-lab dissection. Then he put on sterile gloves and a disposable face mask. He told me to open wide, grabbed my right cheek, took a cotton swab dipped in some unidentifiable, orange-colored cleansing liquid, and wiped the insides of my upper and lower gums. Then he started to bobble the inside of my cheek back and forth. As he did, the professor handed him the most godawful large glass syringe attached to a four-inch needle. I saw him grinning behind the mask, as he jammed that damned needle into my right upper gum and then my lower gum. I started to rise out of the chair, but the professor pushed me back down. In two seconds, the entire right side of my face sagged.

"Mr. Tilden, go easy on the Novocain! A little too much that time."

He bobbled my left cheek and administered a third and fourth piercing. The professor had taken the precaution of going behind my chair and using his arms to restrain me.

Now my entire face felt like a Sharpei dog's. I tried to talk but sounded like a drowning man. Even my tongue was numb.

"Dr. Sommerfield, what size extractor do you recommend for someone with his size mouth?"

I wasn't quite sure how to take that remark.

The old man pointed at the tray, and Pat picked up something more suitable for cutting Romex cable than extracting teeth. He tipped my chair backwards, placed a metal suction tube in my mouth, and jammed a piece of rubber between my upper and lower jaws, so I couldn't close my jaw.

Pat took hold of my right-upper third molar with the pliers, leaned his weight into the chair, and started to wiggle his hand back and forth. On the fourth wiggle my head exploded in a loud "pop," and something flew out of my mouth across the room.

"One down, three to go, Mr. Tilden."

I noticed that the old man was drooling, either with pleasure or from booze.

Three more times I heard the popping sound, and three more times something flew halfway across the clinic room. Meanwhile the suction pump was happily removing a rainbow mixture of blood and saliva from my mouth.

"Galen, I'm going to put some special packing in the holes where your molars were. This will help to protect the openings and allow them to close over correctly."

He returned my chair to the upright position and removed the rubber jaw-stopper and suction tube. I couldn't talk or move my face.

Pat went over to Sommerfield and spoke to him in a low whisper. The old dentist kept staring at me and shaking his head. Then they approached me.

"Mr. Galen, I really should apologize to you. This probably would have gone easier if we had used gas. In any event, I'm going to give you some pain medication to take home. It's a new drug called propoxyphene. It's not a narcotic, so it shouldn't make you sick or goofy."

He handed me a small, brown-plastic bottle.

"Good work, Mr. Tilden. Why don't you walk your friend home?"

Friend?

I still couldn't talk, and I felt a bit weak, as we slowly walked back to the dorm. Along the way I had to keep spitting out the candy-cane-colored saliva that would build up in my mouth, so I could breathe without choking. I opened the door to my room, and Pat put his hand on my shoulder.

"Thanks for doing that, Galen. I'm sorry it turned out to be more than you bargained for. Why don't you just go lie down and rest awhile?"

Yes, I did lie down after he left. About half an hour later I sat straight up. Devils were jabbing pitchforks into both sides of my face. The Novocain had worn off, and I felt like vomiting. I grabbed the little brown bottle and lurched down the hall to the water fountain. The instructions recommended two tablets every six hours. I popped two, sucked up some water, and swallowed hard. Some old blood oozed from my mouth.

It was about twenty feet from the fountain back to my room. I started slowly to avoid jarring my head. I made it to the doorway. Then the lights went out.

I awoke to several voices.

"Is he alright?"

It was Tilden.

"Can you hear me, Mr. Galen?"

I didn't recognize that one.

I opened my eyes. I was lying naked on a gurney, IVs in both arms. I felt something tugging down below and noticed the Foley catheter tube protruding from my urethra. My chest felt like hot pokers had burned me.

They had.

The oxygen mask on my face obscured my words: "What happened?"

The ER resident said, matter-of-factly, "You died."

Tilden pulled a sheet over me, as the orderly began to wheel me from the ER to a holding room. The orderly didn't care if I was naked as a jay bird. He just wanted to get me out of the way, so he could schmooze with the unit secretary.

I shot an angry look at Tilden, and he started to sweat.

"Honest, Galen, I didn't know this would happen. I heard a crash in the hall, and when I came out to see what happened, I found you on the floor. You were turning blue. I pounded on your chest and yelled, until some of the other guys heard me and called the ambulance. They had to shock you. Your heart had stopped.

Okay, scratch propoxyphene from my list of party favors.

You might know it better as Darvon.

They kept me overnight for observation. Even Dave, somewhat exhausted from his afternoon athletic activities with Connie, dropped by. The bed was more comfortable than the prison-style bunk in my dorm room, so I slept fairly well.

I dreamt of Lyman ... Dr. Lyman Lipschutz.

I was eleven going on twelve with all the early pubertal juices in full flow.

One Sunday I had hung around with my friends after church then ate a quick lunch. I wanted to spend the afternoon at Dr. Agnelli's clinic. What an amazing man! He worked seven days a week. God rested on the Sabbath, but not Corrado Agnelli.

That day was quieter than usual—no one else was there. Even the nurses had enough sense to rest.

Dr. Agnelli was sipping from his cup of stale, cold coffee. I had just gotten a cold bottle of Moxie out of the refrigerator and popped off the cap. As I went to take a sip of my favorite nectar, the icy liquid hit my front teeth, and I let out a scream. My left upper bicuspid began to throb in time with my heartbeat.

The good doctor's reflexes were super-fast. He managed to catch the bottle in mid-air, set it down, and catch me, as I started to Z-fold to the floor. He carried me in his arms to a stretcher and gently placed me on it.

I was crying from the pain. I had never felt such agony, even when I had gotten into fights and came out second best. I held the left side of my face as tightly as I could, but it didn't help.

Dr. Agnelli carefully pulled my hand away and told me to open my mouth. The throbbing was intense, but I trusted him more than anyone except Mama and Papa. He took his light and looked inside then took a wooden tongue depressor and looked farther back. Finally he spoke to me.

"Berto, I need to do something that might hurt. I'm going to tap your teeth with the stick. Is that okay with you?"

I wiped away the tears with my right forearm and nodded.

"Listen carefully. This may make the pain flare up. I know you're a brave guy, so you can take it."

You cannot imagine how that comment from my role model made me feel.

I nodded again, and he began to tap slowly. Wise man that he was, he started on the right side and worked his way over to the left. A single contact with that bicuspid caused me to rise and clutch my face.

Dr. Agnelli went to a white-painted, metal-and-glass, floor cabinet, opened it, and took out a small, dark-brown bottle. He unscrewed the lid and removed a dropper. Then he reached for a cotton-tipped stick and put two drops of yellowish liquid on it.

"Open up, Berto. This should help with the pain."

He gently swabbed the gum at the base of the offending tooth, and magically the pain disappeared. I looked at that amazing little bottle. The label said OIL OF CLOVES. From the time I got my first "little black bag" in medical school, I have made sure a bottle of that stuff was in it.

Then Dr. Agnelli did something that surprised me. He went to his telephone and dialed a number.

Strange side thought: It was later, after I had met my friend Edison in high school, that he and I dissected a phone that looked just like the one in Dr. Agnelli's office. We had great fun that day, watching the contact points open and close like little fingers on a player piano, as we turned the dial.

Dr. Agnelli smiled, as a foreign-sounding voice answered loud enough for me to hear across the room. What intrigued me even more was his greeting.

"*Shalom*, Lyman!"

A laugh echoed from the other end "Have you had your *bris* yet, Corrado?"

"The same day you share a ham sandwich with me, Lyman."

Dr. Agnelli looked at me and blushed. I didn't know what the hell the other guy was talking about, so I shrugged my shoulders, and he relaxed.

"Lyman, I have a young man here with a tooth problem. It's no longer *Shabat*, so will you see him? I can be over in ten minutes."

"Yah, yah, bring the boy over," the voice said.

"You feel well enough to walk a block or so, Berto?"

That magic oil was still working, so I nodded. I was getting too big to ride on his shoulders anyway—but I'll bet even today he would have carried me if necessary.

Dr. Agnelli flipped a small sign on the door from OPEN to CLOSED and hung a second one below it: BACK SHORTLY. He locked the door, and we walked slowly down the street. Dr. Agnelli could walk faster than most people run, but he didn't want the impact of walking to jar my tooth.

We turned the block and came upon a row of brownstones with emergency fire escapes hanging from their upper floors. I noticed one of the windows had milk-white, opaque glass with black letters painted on it: LYMAN LIPSCHUTZ, D.D.S. DENTIST.

We entered the building through a wood door painted spruce green and climbed the rickety stairs to the second floor. The oak floorboards were warped and worn and in desperate need of refinishing. The only door with any light on was down the hall. The frosted glass on it carried the same message as the outside window.

Dr. Agnelli knocked then entered. I followed him into a waiting room smelling of tobacco, sweat, and long-past-rancid furniture polish. Before we could sit in one of the circa-1900, mahogany-colored, leather chairs, a gray-haired and bearded figure appeared from a door in the rear.

"*Shalom*, Corrado, this is the boy?"

"Yes. Lyman this is Berto Galen. Berto, this is Dr. Lyman Lipschutz. He is a wonderful dentist. He has saved my teeth many times."

They shook hands, Dr. Agnelli towering over the other man. Even I, not quite twelve, was taller. Then Dr. Lipschutz took my hands in his, and I felt the gnarled irregularity of his bones. I also saw facial scars barely concealed by the beard and found myself wondering what the black, broadcloth suit he wore concealed. I noted his hesitant, dipping, wide-based gait, bow-legged but not from birth.

What had happened to this man?

"Come, boy, we'll look at your teeth."

Dr. Lipschutz led me by the hand into the back room, and Dr. Agnelli followed.

"Here, sit, boy."

He regarded me with a lop-sided grin then said, "Yes, yes, you must be Berto. My friend Corrado has told me much about you."

My mentor nodded. I sat in the chair.

The little dentist whirled a white sheet like a bullfighter and placed it around my chest and under my neck. He pulled a two-step ladder next to the chair and climbed up on it. Next he took my chin, said "open wide," and peered in my mouth.

"Corrado, hand me those gloves."

Dr. Agnelli handed him a pair of dark-brown rubber gloves, and he slipped them on.

"Tell me when it hurts."

He stuck a gloved finger into my mouth and began to wiggle each tooth separately. As he did so, I started to tense up, as he approached what had given me such pain.

"Easy, Berto, easy."

He started to sing softly in a language I later learned was Yiddish, and suddenly I rose from the chair as THE TOOTH lit me up.

He turned to Corrado.

"Bad bicuspid. Good thing it is a baby tooth. Needs to come out."

"Gas?" Dr. Agnelli asked.

"Yah."

He looked me in the eye.

"Berto, that tooth is bad. It needs to come out. That's the bad news. The good news is you have a good tooth underneath. It's due to grow up, just as you will, fairly soon. Will you let Dr. Lipschutz help you?"

I don't know what dentists would have done today. I suspect that the baby tooth would not have been pulled. But then . . . well, that's how it was done. At least that's how it was done in a tenement neighborhood, where the only time one saw a dentist was after it was too late for preventive techniques.

The other thing that startles me: Today, if Dr. Agnelli had taken a child to a dentist without parental permission, he would have become lawyer bait. Back then, he was a hero, an American Mother Teresa. If a child was injured, he would fix the wound—then call the parents. In our neighborhood, there were no phones, so such a message would be sent by shank's mare.

Dr. Agnelli looked at me again.

"Berto, Dr. Lipschutz is going to let you breathe some special air. It's called nitrous oxide. It will make you feel funny, and you might even laugh when you breathe it. It will make you sleepy and you won't feel anything when he removes your tooth. Okay?"

I was sweating in places I didn't know could sweat, but I nodded again.

The little man stepped down off the stool and went to a wheeled gadget that held two tanks of different colors. He pulled it over, stepped up again, and held out a black, rubber triangle attached to two hoses connected to the tanks.

"Corrado, would you hold this to our young man's face?"

Dr. Agnelli moved to my left side and took the mask in his hands.

"Berto, when Dr. Lipschutz turns on the tanks, I'm going to hold this to your face. I want you to take as big a breath as you can and keep breathing."

I heard the hissing, as Dr. Lipschutz turned the knobs and eyed the pressure gauges. Dr. Agnelli held the black mask against my face, and I took a big breath. Within seconds I was floating and giggling. Then things just seemed ... white.

I heard the dentist saying, "He is on full oxygen now," and the room came back into focus. I ran my tongue over where my tooth had been and felt nothing. It was over.

I guess, by today's standards, those two men had committed malpractice and assault and battery on a minor. But back then it was a *mitzva* and a life-saver for me.

I still felt a bit strange. As Dr. Lipschutz returned my chair to the sitting position, his shirtsleeve rose up, and I spied a long number tattooed in dark blue on the inside of his left forearm.

"Lyman, I'll settle the bill with you now."

Dr. Agnelli reached for his wallet, but my gray-haired savior shook his head and touched his friend's shoulder.

"You owe me nothing. It is I who owe you."

My mind was gradually coming back to earth. What a high oxygen deprivation can produce!

Then my tongue went into gear before my common sense did.

"Dr. Lipschutz, what's that number on your arm?"

He appeared quite startled by my question. He began to shake. His arms clutched his chest, and he began to rock back and forth, as his face melted in tears.

Dr. Agnelli threw his arms around Dr. Lipschutz and held him to his chest. His own face creased in empathy for the dentist's grief. I had never seen him like this. His quiet voice resonated in the stillness of the dental operatory.

"Berto, Lyman survived Auschwitz."

Dr. Lipschutz's voice then crooned words I did not understand.

"Me hot zey in dr'erd, me vet zey iberlebn, me vet noch derlebn."

To hell with them, we will survive them, we will yet survive.

Now that scarred face and twisted mouth continued to speak, its eyes lit with fire, its voice no longer trembling. Dr. Lipschutz sang louder and louder—and then he stopped.

"No, boy, I am not crazy. You are Christian. You had your martyred Nazarene carpenter. Our murdered carpenter was my friend, Mordecai Gebertig."

Dr. Agnelli loosened his arms, and he shook himself like a dog shaking off rainwater. His eyes, dark brown dissolving to black, burned with a frightful intensity.

"Sit, Berto, sit."

Dr. Agnelli nodded to me.

"Berto, hear me and learn. Someday, when you are old, you will remember Lyman, yes? You will remember my words."

Lipschutz used the footstool to climb up on a side counter facing the dental chair I once again occupied—this time only to listen. Dr. Agnelli boosted himself onto another counter, and we both gazed at the little man who was now more alive than anyone else in the room.

"I was not always like this, Berto. What you see, what I am now, was created by devils masquerading as men."

His face twitched, and I held my breath, hoping he would not descend into that pit of despair as before.

"No, Berto, once I was tall, almost like Corrado."

His mouth split into an awful grin.

"I was good looking, too, my friend, not like you."

Dr. Agnelli chuckled, but Dr. Lipschutz's voice quavered.

"And then my Krakow, my beautiful Krakow, was invaded by brutes.

"It was *Ha-Shoah.*"

The Holocaust.

Juden verboten! Juden verboten!

No Jews allowed.

"Even now I can see the signs and hear the shouts."

He turned to Dr. Agnelli.

"Corrado, my friend, why do men become devils?"

He did not answer.

The dentist shook his head to cast away memories.

"I was born in Krakow, Poland, in 1910."

I stared in disbelief. It meant that his shriveled presence was only forty-one!

Once more he grinned.

"My papa was a merchant. My mama loved my papa and raised me and my three brothers. They all went into Papa's business.

"I was the youngest and the most spoiled, so I put on airs of being a doctor or a dentist. I actually won a scholarship to attend a prestigious dental school in Germany—and I could speak German better than any Aryan son of Herman!"

He pointed to the large, elaborate diploma hanging on the wall. It was marked COPY, and Dr. Agnelli sensed my question coming.

"Remember, Berto, everything is destroyed by war."

He whispered hoarsely, as he stared at the wall.

"Yes... my mama, my papa, my brothers... and me!

"No, Berto, I did not look like this back then. Once I was tall and straight, and my face was admired and stroked by all the ladies. I was quite the swain once upon a time.

"And then they came. It was 1939. They walled us up, thousands of us, in a section of Krakow meant to hold only hundreds. They did not want to defile their precious Aryan eyes with the sight of Jews.

"We were demoralized. We tried to maintain our dignity, what little autonomy we had in our kennel existence. But our conquerors, the racial purifiers, who perverted everything they touched, could not allow that. Their efforts were deliberate and concerted. We were to be broken, turned into the animals they said we were."

I shuddered, and the two men saw it.

I was a boy on the verge of manhood. I had seen violence and death in my tenement neighborhood, but my young mind could not fathom the depths of depravity that this man, Lyman Lipschutz, had endured. It was all I could do not to shout to Dr. Agnelli, "Did this really happen?"

Dr. Lipschutz understood my thoughts. He removed his shirt.

"See, boy. They broke my arms, my legs, my back! My jaw met the butt end of a rifle many times.

"My friends—those who took gas 'showers'—they were the lucky ones."

I closed my eyes. I couldn't stand the sight. There was no normal skin.

I kept my eyes closed, as Dr. Lipschutz described how some in the Krakow Ghetto had tried to maintain the human spirit; how his friend Mordecai Gebertig, a carpenter by trade, a balladeer by talent, had been punished by the Nazis for keeping hope alive with his songs: The monsters had silenced his music with a bullet.

Dr. Agnelli jumped down from his counter seat and went to his friend. I heard his whispered words.

"Lyman, you don't have to do this. The boy has heard enough."

"No! No, he must hear, he must learn! This will happen again. The beast within us all can resurface, no matter how civilized we think we are."

As Dr. Agnelli knew he would, the dentist began to sob once more, so he held him again ... and cried with him.

I am an old man now. I have seen life and death, in myriad ways, many times. To this day my psyche cannot comprehend the enormity of Lipschutz's words.

But, Lyman, I do not forget.

The Junk Man

Nothing is ever as it seems.

"Dr. Galen, you have three more patients to see."

I was doing a month's rotation in the medical clinics my senior year. The school provided the clinics to the indigent poor and those barely managing to scrape by on what little they earned. Even the medications were free. All a patient had to do was deal with someone like me—not yet a doctor and desperately trying to learn by practicing on a real person.

The standing joke back then: What do a mortician, a pathologist, and a student seeing patients at the clinic have in common?

Answer: None of their clients could complain about the service.

On that particular day I had finished the first two patients quickly—nothing major, just nice, simple sore throats and runny noses—and then walked into the third examining room. It was barely the size of a broom closet, but it held two chairs and an exam table that probably had seen service in the Spanish-American War.

I looked at the entry data sheet the nurse had handed me and put on my best "concerned look." They taught us how to look concerned, but I'm not sure it made any difference.

"Hello, Mr. Allman, I'm Dr. Galen. What seems to be the problem?"

He was a middle-aged man, his hands slightly shaky, and his sallow complexion rimmed with sun-pink face. As I got nearer, I could smell the mixed perfume of stale body sweat and even staler beer.

He looked me over, all shiny and scrubbed, wearing my student whites, and sighed. To him I might as well have been a kid dressed as a doctor for Halloween. He knew he wouldn't be seeing a "real doctor."

I steeled myself. I wasn't that far from graduation. Soon I could legitimately call myself "Dr. Galen," even though I still knew next to nothing about the human condition.

I went for the honesty gambit.

"Yes, sir, I know. I'm a medical student, but I can call in one of our staff doctors to see you, after I do some initial evaluation."

That only partly reversed his disappointment, so I tried again.

"What kind of work do you do?"

"I'm a garbage man, Doc," and his face actually broke a smile.

I sat down beside him.

"That's hard work. What brings you here?"

The worry in his eyes was palpable. I already had jumped to the conclusion that he was an alcoholic. After all, he was shaky and giving off a pretty strong aroma. I sensed that he wanted to talk.

"I'm getter weaker, Doc. Look at me."

I did. I guessed he was about five-feet ten, but under a-hundred-and-forty pounds, which turned out to be correct when I measured and weighed him.

"Doc, I used to weigh about a-hundred-and-eighty pounds. I could lift cans and containers that weighed as much as I did, and it didn't bother me. Then, about two months ago, I started to get real hot all of a sudden. I couldn't control my peeing. I started to get the shakes."

He looked down at the floor, his face in full blush with embarrassment.

"I was no good with my wife … if you know what I mean."

He stopped talking.

"Is that when you started drinking?"

He seemed relieved.

"Yeah, the booze helped the shakes and my headaches at first, then…"

Headaches? What the hell was I dealing with? My mind raced, as I threw out another question.

"Anyone else in your family have any problems like this?"

"Yeah, my dad died young. They said it was a stroke."

"How old was he?"

"My age, forty-two."

All you medically savvy folks, I know what you're thinking: Get those big chemistry panels and some MRIs and total-body scans on this guy. That would've been great, but we had no such fancy devices or instant lab tests in the Jurassic period when I attended med school. I actually had to listen to my patient, examine him and—heaven forbid—put my hands on his body.

I took his blood pressure—two hundred over one ten, with a resting pulse rate above a hundred beats per minute! His heart was racing, and his skin was clammy. His neck felt lumpy. I started to suspect exophthalmos from too much of the thyroid-related hormones, but his eyes weren't bulging—yep, a fancy word meaning popeyed.

While he lay on that antique examining table, stripped to his shorts, I moved my fingers over his belly, checking for masses and enlarged blood vessels or organs. Nothing stood out.

Damn, this can't be just simple overactive thyroid and diabetes!

Then one of those rare epiphanies of mind and intellect hit me. The letters MEN popped into my head: multiple endocrine neoplasia. It's a typical mouthful of words we docs like to invent.

Roughly translated it means sometimes the human body decides to run amok, not just in one gland but in several. No question this guy had an overactive thyroid, probably due to a type of tumor, but his shakes and headaches, sweating and weight loss were being caused by small glands that sit on top of the kidneys called the adrenals. Get a tumor there and all hell breaks loose.

Small as they are, the adrenal glands produce the hormones that control our well-being: cortisol and adrenalin. A tumor of the adren-alin-producing cells, called a pheochromocytoma, can kill a person with massive spikes of circulating adrenalin. The blood pressure and pulse go through the ceiling, you get headaches, and then you stroke out.

"Go ahead and get dressed, Mr. Allman. I want to call one of the staff doctors in to confirm what I think is going on. I have a feeling you're going to be admitted for testing."

"Doc, I don't have any money."

"Yeah, I know that. You still need to come in. I'll call the social worker after the attending sees you."

I spoke with the senior clinic doctor out in the hallway. He shook his head in disbelief.

"Pheos are pretty rare, Galen."

As we entered the examining room, he patted me on the shoulder.

"Listen, kid, when you hear hoof beats, it's most likely a horse and not a zebra."

After he had finished checking out Allman, he turned to me and muttered, "I'll be damned!"

I won't tell you about the primitive tests our poor patient had to en-dure to confirm my suspicions. I don't want to make you nauseous. Suffice it to say I was right, and I was elated, as I returned to my apart-ment that evening. Every good medical student dreams of making that rare diagnosis, finding the zebra instead of the horse, when those hoof-beats thunder in your ears.

I was exhausted but happy. I lay down—just for a minute, you understand—and as I drifted off to sleep in my street clothes, I recalled Giuseppe.

I was fifteen, a sophomore at Concepción High School. I had managed to finish the hefty pile of homework the good nuns and lay teachers had assigned us for fun on a beautiful spring weekend.

I kissed Mama, as I headed down the stairs of our tenement building.

Where was I going? Out!

It was midday Saturday and Sal—my friend Salvatore—waited for me. He and my other friends, Angie and Tomas, had gone on to the local public high school, after we graduated from St. Mary's grammar school. I was lucky enough to get a scholarship to the Catholic high school in a nearby town.

Angie and Tomas were no longer in high school. Their new and permanent home was the little cemetery at the edge of our neighborhood. Sal and I carried on without them.

"Hey, *Dottore* Berto, kill anyone today?"

Sal was bigger and a helluva lot stronger than I was, but he was the friendliest, puppy-dog person you ever met. Behind that broad, dopey smile was a mind far sharper than mine.

He just didn't realize it.

"Hey, Sal, where ya wanna go?"

After five days of speaking properly at school, I easily reverted to our neighborhood patois.

"Where else? Giuseppe's!"

Giuseppe Monteverdi. We called him the Clip-Clop Man.

He also went by the name of Joe, and he was the neighborhood junk man. Monday through Saturday, the scarecrow-tall Joe would hook up his old, dappled mare to the wooden wagon with the name JOE'S JUNK painted on the sides. Up and down our neighborhood, and then outward to more affluent territories, he would scour the place for scrap metal, bits of wood, and other castaways of daily living.

Funny. Back in those days, recycling was natural, because people were so poor that anything of value was used and reused. In our community, nothing ever got thrown out—except drunken husbands, unfaithful wives, or reprobate kids.

For me, outside of the pigeons, packs of roaming dogs, and one special old alley cat, that dappled mare was as close to nature as we ever got.

Clip-clop, clip-clop, clip-clop.

Anytime we heard that sound we ran to it, laughing and pushing each other, trading jokes in puberty-cracked voices about the girls we knew. If you could believe Sal, the girls in public school had the girls at my Catholic school beat hands down for looks—and other things.

Thinking back, I'm not so sure. Yes, they were forced to wear the ugliest plaid skirts this side of Scotland, but there were some genuine lookers, and they were smart, too. What used to tee me off was that Sal usually had at least two coeds hanging from his shoulders, while I held up the gym wall at dances.

I admit it. I was a bit envious.

Clip-clop, clip-clop, clip-clop.

The wagon was just turning onto Grand. When we caught up with it, Sal leaped onto the open back and gave me, huffing behind, one of his famous, one-armed boosts. He was so strong.

I was laughing and gasping for air, when I heard the Voice.

"Watch out for those glass shards, guys."

Giuseppe sounded like a bumblebee. If you remember those strangely vibrating, androgynous voices in the old space-alien flicks, that was Monteverdi. The only time I was able to imitate him was at university, when I inhaled helium gas from a balloon on a dare.

"Hey, Giuseppe, get any good loot yet?"

Sal had turned toward the old man sitting like Ichabod Crane on the driver's bench, his long legs splayed out over the rims of the buckboard.

"Whoa, girl. Whoa!"

The horse stopped and did what stopped horses usually do.

In our neighborhood, it was never picked up—it was eventually consumed by the flies or washed away by the rain.

"Got my eye on some stuff over on..."

I listened to the banter between Giuseppe and Sal, as he related how he had spotted some "stuff" over in the "rich" section.

"You guys wanna help me load it? Two bits fer each o' ya."

"Hey, Giuseppe, this sure as hell beats walkin'. You game, Berto?"

"Sure."

I didn't have to be home for a while.

Besides, two bits was a fortune.

Clip-clop, clip-clop, clip-clop.

Strange. I didn't think of it back then, but a certain incongruity hits me now that I'm almost plant food: If I was such a smart kid, why didn't I think it unusual to see Giuseppe over in the rich section sometimes without his horse and wagon? And why did he waste time in our little slice of heaven, where there was nothing to be had?

We passed the local row of storefronts. We waved at Mr. Ruddy in his shoe-repair shop and Mr. Huff in his electrical-motor shop. As we passed the candy lady's place, Giuseppe turned and spat a cud of tobacco chaw onto her sidewalk, while Sal and I laughed and clapped.

I still missed Bernice.

I could see Thomas the Barber cutting someone's hair. He gave us a left-handed wave without missing a beat, as those magic fingers on his right hand kept doing their snip-snip click with his scissors. I would stop by later and sweep out his store and talk about school before heading over to Dr. Agnelli's clinic.

Even the air changed as we turned off the main street. The sunlight was brighter, the sky a deeper blue, as we entered "their" neighborhood. "They" were the ones who made things happen—using the labor of our parents. They lived in individual brick homes with detached garages to store their vehicles. Their streets and driveways sported the latest, 1954-model cars.

It was the dawn of the tailfin age—shiny metal beasts in all shades of primary colors and pastels. We even saw a few of those fabulous, Batmobile Corvettes that always brought a gleam to Sal's eyes.

"See that, Berto? Someday I'm gonna have one o' those."

He pointed at a low-slung, fire-engine-red convertible that seemed to be moving even while parked.

"Sure, Sal, and I'm gonna be a famous doctor who refuses to see you 'cause you stink!"

Needless to say, underarm deodorants were not within the budgets of most of us back then. He gave me a friendly punch on the shoulder, which I felt for a week afterward.

Clip-clop, clip-clop, clip-clop.

"Here she is boys, the mother lode!"

Giuseppe guided the wagon next to the curb in front of a huge home that I later learned was called Tudor style. Back then all I knew was it looked bigger than the little church attached to our old grammar school.

Sitting on the sidewalk was furniture of all descriptions: tables, couches, dining-room chairs, lounge chairs, bookcases, and stuff I didn't recognize. I wasn't sure the old wagon could haul it all, much less the poor horse pulling it.

"Come on, Berto, we're gonna earn two bits!"

Sal jumped down, and I followed. We stood in awe, running our hands over brocaded upholstery—something else I learned about later—and smooth, dark-wood tables so shiny we could see our faces in the tops. I couldn't take my eyes off a small desk and chair with a bookcase beside it. Sal plopped himself in a padded armchair and pretended to smoke a stogie.

"Ain't got all day, guys. Git a move on!"

One did not disobey the bumblebee.

We loaded the wagon from stem to stern.

"Hey, we didn't do too bad a job, Berto."

"Sal, where we gonna sit?"

"Hop up here, boys. There's room on the bench. I might even let ya ride old Mandy, here."

Our eyes widened, and our jaws dropped. Giuseppe never let anyone ride the old mare. We hopped up and squeezed next to him. He reached into his pocket and bit off another tobacco chaw then held it out to us.

Sal winked at me. He took the stick and bit off a piece. I shook my head. I already had seen too many sick smokers and chewers at Dr. Agnelli's clinic.

"Giddap, old girl."

Clip-clop, clip-clop, clip-clop.

I caught the movement out of the corner of my left eye. A woman stood looking out the big picture window of that castle-sized house. She smiled and waved. I saw Giuseppe, hand low down, wave back.

"O-h-h, I don't feel so good!"

Sal looked green around the gills. Good thing he was sitting on the edge of the bench. He leaned over and puked, until his face turned amber.

Giuseppe laughed.

"Want another chaw, kid?"

Sal leaned over and puked again.

"Who wants to ride Mandy?"

Now Sal didn't look so interested.

Giuseppe pulled back on the reins and let out a "Whoa!"

"Go ahead, Berto."

I wasn't the most athletic kid. Hell, I was lucky I could finish running laps in gym. But I hopped down and used the trace holders to boost myself up on that poor horse's rump. Then I slid myself forward and stroked her head. She turned around to me.

"Ready?"

"Yes, sir!"

Sal seemed to be recovering. He let out a sickly laugh.

"Okay, Hopalong *Che cosa dite*. Let's see you stay on that horse!"

Monteverdi flicked the reins, and off we went.

Clip-clop, clip-clop, clip-clop.

At first I was scared out of my gourd. I kept whispering in that horse's ear, "Don't make me fall."

Eventually, I calmed down and sat straight up—though I still held tight to Mandy's neck mane.

We entered the old neighborhood in triumph. I kept yelling, "Hi yo, Silver," and waving to folks we knew. I looked like a total idiot.

Giuseppe pulled the wagon to the curb in front of the candy lady's store.

"Thanks fer helpin' out, guys. Here…"

He flipped quarters to Sal and me. I slid off the horse's back. By then I didn't want to leave her. Sal jumped down from the seat.

"Sure you don't need us to unload this stuff, Giuseppe?"

"Naw, thanks."

I shot a longing look at the little desk set and bookcase. Sal was even more obvious. He really liked that armchair.

Giuseppe just said "giddap!"

As the horse pulled away, we noticed what it had left in front of the candy lady's store.

Sal said he had something to do, so I headed to see Thomas the

Barber. My legs were a bit sore from clenching the sides of the old mare. My rump felt even worse, but I wouldn't have traded that ride for anything.

It was almost closing time. I walked in and picked up the broom lying in the back of the barber shop. Thomas looked me over and wrinkled his nose.

"Phew! Berto, you smell like horse!"

He was smiling. He had seen me riding and playing the fool.

"Thomas ever tell you 'bout time he rode Siberian pony? I go see girl with big bazookas while her papa out and he come back early and..."

"Yes, Thomas, you did."

"I tell you how hard is put clothes on while horse gallop? Pants worst."

"Yes, Thomas."

"I tell you how papa shoot gun at Thomas?"

"Uh, yes."

I finished sweeping. Thomas went to his ice box, pulled out a beer and a Moxie, handed me the soda pop, and sat down in one of the barber chairs.

"So, how you like horse, Berto?"

What could I say? To this day I remember the look in the beast's big brown eyes. I really think it understood what I was saying. Yes, even now I have a soft spot for large, dumb animals.

A thought pops into my head: Giuseppe never used a whip.

Thomas and I guzzled down our drinks and tried to outdo each other belching. He won.

It's a guy thing. Actually it's a boy thing—it's just that some boys don't give it up.

I headed to the clinic. It was still daylight, and it was Saturday, Agnelli's busiest day—and night. I had gotten permission from Mama and Papa to stay late.

The candy lady's store was on my way. As I passed by, I saw her using a snow shovel to scoop up Mandy's little gift to the street. I actually felt sorry for the old woman, even though I couldn't stand her. She was so miserable.

"Can I help you with that, ma'am?"

She stood up straight. I could almost hear her joints creak. She stared at me then spat out, "You go tell that degenerate old man if that horse of his does this again, I'll shoot it—and him!"

I kept on going.

Mr. Huff's store lights were out. Sure enough, he was in Mr. Ruddy's place next door. The two Old Guys were chewing the fat as I passed. Mr. Ruddy waved at me to come in.

"Berto, you gonna be a cowboy now, huh? What's poor old Agnelli gonna thinka that? We all figgered you was gonna take over his place in a coupla years."

Mr. Huff tried to wink, but that World War One shellshock trauma sent his face into a grotesque spasm.

Mr. Ruddy swung his half-body onto the counter. His bright-blue eyes were creased with laugh lines.

"You know, Berto, I had dreams once. See, after the war I was gonna stay in the army and become a cavalry officer. Always did like horses, and I heard the military was gonna set up a whole new cavalry brigade."

He raised his head and grinned.

"I'd sure look damned funny if I tried that now, don'tcha think?"

Mr. Huff swigged his beer, belched, and laughed.

"Harry, you could get one a them hookah things all them sultans used ta ride in. Don't need any legs!"

His face spasmed again.

Both men looked at the floor. I tried to break the silence.

"It was a helluva lotta fun riding Mandy."

"Watch yer mouth, boy! You're not allowed to cuss yet. That's just for old farts like us. Besides, if you're gonna be a sawbones like Agnelli some day ... well, docs don't cuss."

He was right. Dr. Agnelli never cussed.

Harry, if you're up there in heaven, and you're conscious of this old man's ramblings, I can tell you stories about docs and cussing that would curl your wings. I don't know if I'm going to wind up where you guys are now, but even if my afterlife is a lot warmer, we can still talk, can't we?

Both men could see I was embarrassed, so Mr. Huff pointed to the refrigerator and said "Grab a soda pop, kid."

I grabbed a Moxie and leaned against the counter—I was having a drink with the Old Guys!

"Did you know Old Joe was a horseman in the army?"

I looked at Mr. Ruddy with a start.

"Yep, old Joe, he's older than us, kid. He's gotta be pushin' seventy. He was in the cavalry down on the Tex-Mex border chasing Pancho Villa under Black Jack Pershing. Some damned bandito shot him off his horse and stuck a knife in his throat."

Mr. Huff finished the story.

"Joe's horse stayed by his side, 'til he was rescued."

They watched the understanding spread across my face.

That explained the Voice.

"Old Joe used to be quite a lady's man. He even dated that Donnelly woman. 'Course her name was Lottie Smith. She was hot stuff then."

He stopped and grinned.

Mr. Huff took a turn.

"Yeah, me, Harry, Tim, Titus and Tommy, we kids used ta sneak behind her and lift the back o' her petticoats. Harry, didn't she give Tommy a whack on the head with her fancy parasol?"

Mr. Ruddy laughed.

"Yeah, she did! Then Titus snatched it from her and ran down the street singing in falsetto!"

Now both men were busting a gut.

"Old Joe, he finally got smart and realized what he was dealing with, so he took off. Left her for a pretty Mexican girl he met just over the border. The old biddy never forgave him. She had to settle for Shamus Donnelly."

I recognized the name from whispered gossip when I was younger. Old Shamus was the neighborhood sloppy drunk. One day he wound up facedown dead in front of one of the local bars.

Funny how the memory plays tricks as you age. The only image that comes to mind of the candy lady now is a mixture of "American Gothic" and "The Scream."

"Mr. Huff, how did Joe get into the junk business?"

My face must have looked stupid-innocent, because both men laughed so hard at my question they would have rolled on the floor if they could.

"Joe, he's one smart cookie. He went down to Texas. Did some straw boss work and bought property. Guess what? That property had oil on it!"

Mr. Ruddy nodded.

"Where'd we go wrong, George? How come we ain't rich?"

Some secret joke passed between them.

As the sun got ready to set, I thanked the men for the soda pop and headed to the clinic.

Dr. Agnelli looked tired. With each year the work load got bigger, and he got older. I tried to help out as best I could without getting in his way. He let me do some of the minor stuff, albeit under his hawk-eyed supervision. I helped set fractures and clean minor wounds. I actually got pretty good at simple procedures.

The first thing Dr. Agnelli said when he saw me was, "Berto, go put on some scrubs. You stink!"

Damn, how come I couldn't smell it?

I learned the physiology much later: It's a defense mechanism—the brain tends to ignore the body's own odors, so it can pick up the scents of others.

It was after eleven p.m. when things settled down. Dr. Agnelli wisely allowed some of the really late-night cases to go to the hospital. He couldn't handle the escalating trauma coming out of the neighborhood. He was a miracle worker, but he was still human, and he recognized the increasing need for rest periods.

In med school and residency they beat such common sense out of you. It takes years to realize how stupid it is to acquire a god complex.

We batted small talk for a while, and then he stood up and said, "Let's call it a night."

Four weeks passed. It was nearing the end of the school year, and everyone was cramming for finals. I doubt that was Sal's case, but he wasn't around even when I did have some breathing time. So I started a habit I have kept ever since: I took long walks.

I walked and walked and walked. Most times I really didn't know where I was going or why. I just ambled.

That day I was ambling past the storefronts of my friends, including Mr. Buck's. I saw a new sign in the window: B&C'S WATCH AND CLOCK REPAIR.

I hadn't noticed that before. The door was open, so I stuck my head in. The old man and the young man sat at the workbench: Mr. Buck and Paolo Cherubini.

I hadn't seen Paolo since grammar school. He wasn't the same little kid I knew. Puberty does that.

He was almost as tall as I was, and his face was still weird looking, but it showed something I and most of my friends didn't have: contentment.

Neither looked up, so focused were they on those tiny gears and levers and pinions.

I left the store as quietly as I could.

Corrado, my mentor, my friend, would we have done the same if you had lived after I graduated medical school?

I walked to the end of my world and into the world that was "Theirs."

I still wasn't sure what I was doing, walking without gawking at the American Taj Mahals, their elaborate, sculpted-metal beasts on four wheels parked out in front awaiting the whims of their masters. I saw well-dressed people, well-fed people. None of them showed the contentment that Paolo's face had displayed.

I passed the house where my Marigold Lady once lived.

Are you content now, Lady?

Suddenly I noticed I had neared the big, Tudor-style mansion. I hadn't really studied it the last time, being too busy and overwhelmed by the treasure of furniture so casually disposed of.

Wrought-iron fencing surrounded the house. A large, ornate, double metal gate lay open, exposing a block-long driveway that curved both in front and to the rear. There was a manicured lawn with numerous, flowering bushes—azaleas—which I later cultivated at my Virginia home, filling in the front and sides. Several well-kept flowerbeds, adorned with early and mid season tulips, had been strategically placed around dwarf trees and a garden fountain.

It was far too large to be Hansel and Gretel's enchanted cottage, but I stood there in the driveway, enraptured by the sheer beauty of it all. I didn't snap out of my reverie for several minutes. Then, as I turned and began to walk back the way I had come, my ears heard what my mind refused to believe:

From the back of the house came the distinct sounds of a neighing horse and a human bumblebee calling out, "Easy, old girl, easy."

The Working Girl

They're known by many names.

For those of you who haven't had the pleasure of spending a typical night in a hospital emergency room, let me be your guide. I was finishing my junior year in medical school and beginning the first of three rotations in emergency service. It was daunting. We shifted back and forth between two distinct units, one medical, and the other surgical/trauma.

Yes, I had already seen more than most as a boy, helping Dr. Agnelli at his clinic in the tenements. Those weekend crushes with patients milling around, people assaulted by various injuries and illnesses, proved invaluable if difficult experiences. They pulled at you, demanding treatment as adults while descending into childlike dependence and fear—I had taken it all in.

But this latter day Gehenna exceeded anything I had encountered back home by logarithmic magnitudes, including the Saturday Night Knife and Gun Club types, or the poor souls staring blankly with alcohol- or drug-glazed eyes. Those cases involved people making stubborn and repeated bad judgments, and receiving a bullet hole or knife wound—or self-induced stupor—as a result.

Here, it was the sheer number and utter starkness of the dead, fatalities caused by riding in moving vehicles that had suddenly met immovable objects or, maybe, someone at the wrong place at the wrong time, a piece of industrial equipment rending the body, or an individual suffering unspeakable cruelty at the hand of a family member or lover. Sometimes they lay by the dozens on carts along the wall, the deceased among the living and injured.

My ears rang with the moans and outbursts of screams, and the sobbing of family members standing by a lost son or daughter, imploring whatever deities they believed in to bring their loved ones back. It was a scene from "Dante's Inferno."

"Galen, we'll start you off easy."

I couldn't be sure if the ER surgical resident was serious or joking. His face was inscrutable, something I later saw out in the field as well. It was the mind's self-defense against horror delivered on a daily basis. It was shell shock, PTSD—you name it.

He handed me a clipboard with an attached admission form. The admitting nurse had filled it in:

LAST NAME: Stanley

FIRST NAME: Billy

AGE: 15

RACE: White

SEX: Male

The rest of the form was blank, except for big red letters rubber-stamped across the bottom:

DOA

"Hit and run," the resident muttered. "He was trying to cross a highway and got clipped. The bastard never stopped to help him. You need to tell the family. All they know is that the kid's here."

He turned and walked away. A nurse guided him to someone he could actually help.

I walked into ER Bay 3 and lifted the sheet to look at the teenager lying on the gurney cart. He was wearing what we then called dungarees—blue jeans now—and Keds sneakers. No, make that one Keds sneaker. His left foot was shoeless. The red-plaid shirt he had put on earlier that day was torn and bloody. His left leg was sitting at a severely unnatural angle.

Then I looked at his face.

It wasn't there.

His head was a giant, purple grape that had been rolled over by a tire carrying a two-ton vehicle.

Where his hair should have formed dark brown waves, gray-white and bloodied tissue protruded like a mushroom.

"Where's Billy, where's my Billy?"

I turned at the sound of the woman's voice. Reflexively I re-covered the boy, just before she entered the bay. When she saw the sheet-draped body, she collapsed to the floor.

The man who had walked in with her helped me to seat her in a nearby chair. He looked at me. I knew that he knew.

"May I see him?"

"Uh … sir … I … uh … I don't recommend it. He was just brought in."

He stared at me, seeing me for the neophyte that I was.

"Son, I'm a doctor. This is my nephew. Please…"

I stood back as he moved toward the cart and slowly raised the sheet. When I heard him gasp, I moved forward to help, but he raised his hand to me and lowered the covering.

The morgue attendant was kind. He waited, until I had guided Billy's family out to the special area, where social workers would assist them through the government-mandated hell of paperwork. Then he pushed the cart into the corridor and headed to the morgue.

I heard him humming a tune from "Show Boat."

My whites soaked with sweat, I walked to the nursing station. I wanted to sit down, but the charge nurse handed me another clipboard and leered at me.

"Don't know why, but the resident said to go easy with you, seeing as how it's your first day. Least this one's alive."

Her face softened.

"You ever deal with a working girl?"

I realize now that the first case had stunned me. All I could give her was a quizzical look.

"Boy, I'm talking about a prossy, a street lady, a lady of the night." A blank stare from me.

"Damn it, boy, a whore!"

I nodded. My childhood tenement neighborhood had its share of red-light ladies.

"From the looks a you, I guess you were never a john." Another stupid look.

"Hell, boy, you know what I mean. You never used one?"

Never did, but I knew about them—Sal had made sure of that.

Once more the nurse got down to business.

"This girl got herself beat up by her pimp. She'll need the full evaluation, including the rape kit—though I don't know what that will prove. You'll need a nurse to chaperone. You done pelvics before?"

I nodded meekly.

"And kid, get outta those whites. Put on some scrubs. You'll be a helluva lot more comfortable."

Crusty old gal, but she was right. From then on it was hospital blues—scrubs—for me in the ER.

I walked into Bay 6, accompanied by a nurse fresh out of training. Her nametag read LUANN. We both stood staring at the woman lying on her side on the cart. I read the admission sheet, with the name and age omitted. The only background information was obvious—she was a white female—but at least the admitting nurse had done a preliminary workup on her:

Multiple contusions and lacerations. Signs of blunt trauma. Possible physical/ sexual abuse.

I later learned her name and age—Ruby Joseph, thirty-five—but she looked much older than that. Like Billy Stanley, she also looked like she had been run over. She had open wounds and bruises on her face, arms, chest, and abdomen. I could see the boot imprints where she had been kicked on her belly and thighs. And there were unusual swellings just below her umbilicus (belly button) and from her rectum.

I introduced myself to her, but she just kept staring at the wall in front of her. She remained silent, as I looked over her head, neck, and chest, making lines on the body diagram on the clipboard to locate her bruises and cuts.

I examined her eyes. Large shiners encircled both sides and the whites of her eyeballs were hemorrhaging. Her chest was a sheet of purple.

Luann gently attempted to roll her onto her back to allow me to check the abdomen and nether regions. But she resisted and suddenly seemed to be in distress. So I palpated her as she lay. I felt the early changes of heavy alcohol consumption in the size and firmness of her liver. Then my hand moved just below her umbilicus. I felt something hard—much too hard for human tissue.

Luann, bless her, had gloved up and was about to try again to roll Ruby onto her back, while I put on gloves and opened the rape kit.

Suddenly the patient jerked and screamed in agony, and as the sheet dropped from her body Luann let out an "omigod!" Then we both saw what was protruding from her front and back.

Someone had inserted empty brown beer bottles deeply into her vagina and anus.

They were lodged so tightly it took both hands to remove them.

I ordered stat (immediate) X-rays of Ruby's abdomen, chest, and head. Ultrasound was still in its infancy, so X-rays were the only way to go. And, yes, we did run a pregnancy test.

We also carefully put the two bottles in evidence bags.

Luann shook her head.

"She's going to need a gynecologist to repair her."

"If she survives," I replied, as we both removed our gloves. Then we heard it:

"Code blue! Code blue! Radiology department."

The loudspeaker squawked the come-hither words that all medical personnel dread. I had a gut feeling, as Luann and I began our inevitable hospital walk, a corridor-eating run to the X-ray department, just behind the intern and surgical resident.

The radiology resident and his student were already pounding on Ruby Joseph's chest. Hard to believe but her face was even bluer than before, and her bruised chest no longer moved in breathing time.

The surgical resident shined his penlight in the patient's eyes. They didn't constrict. Her pupils were dilated. He and the radiology resident both nodded, as the intern said, "Massive PE, probably air."

Whoever had thrust those bottles inside Ruby's rectum and vagina had somehow forced some air inside the large vein in her belly. All it takes is about a quarter cup, and even though it's gaseous, it acts like a solid plug, as it moves up the blood vessels to the right side of the heart—stopping it.

They tried fluoroscope-guided needle aspiration (drainage) of her heart, but Ruby Joseph was gone. Those glass bottles, complete with fingerprints, later served to convict her pimp of manslaughter.

Luann and I were pretty shaken as we returned to the ER. The old charge nurse—her name was Mabel if I recall correctly—took us both aside. She was crusty, but she was also kind. She saw two novices just bludgeoned by the process of sudden death. No amount of training blunts the effect the first time you confront it, and Mabel knew it. I later learned she had served in the army in World War II and had been captured and held by the Japanese in one of their infamous POW camps when the Philippines were invaded.

And about Luann, yes, I started to entertain thoughts of dating her, but I was going steady with my classmate, June, and she was a newlywed.

Time passes, even when you're not having fun. My roommate, Dave, and I had settled into our townhouse apartment up on Church Hill. It was just a quick walk from the hospital complex over an ancient bridge called the Marshall Street Viaduct. Its rickety structure shuddered even in the slightest breeze, but it had spanned the valley between two of the seven hills of Richmond for many years.

I felt tired, as I walked up the driveway to the federally subsidized housing complex and unlocked the front door. Dave had already arrived and had strategically ensconced himself in his favorite room, the bathroom.

"Finish up in there, Country Boy. A better man needs to use the john."

I almost laughed out loud as Mabel's word came to mind.

Then the door knocker sounded.

"Bob, answer the door. I'm not done yet."

I had already taken off my shoes, so I padded down the stairs and looked through the peephole. Mrs. Bailey, our next-door neighbor, stood there.

I opened the door, but she didn't wait for an invitation. She stepped in, dragging a familiar young boy by the arm.

"Now, Marcus Bailey, you tell them doctahs what's wrong!"

"Yes, Mama."

Marcus and his younger brother Jeremiah were good kids, but they sure could get themselves into trouble. Dave and I had to rescue Jeremiah from being entombed inside the upper end of the Chimborazo train tunnel that ran under Church Hill shortly after we moved there.

I squatted down, more because I was tired than needing to go eye to eye with the boy. But that told me what was wrong before Marcus even began to speak. His eyes were tearing, and the white parts were puffy and red.

I stood up and asked his mother the key question.

"Is anyone doing any metal work around here—cutting or welding metal?"

She looked astonished.

"Yeah, coupla blocks over. They's cuttin' rods fer a new buildin'."

I took the boy's right hand in mine.

"Marcus, were you watching a man using a really bright electric light?"

"Yessuh."

I heard the toilet flush, and Dave bounded down the stairs behind me in his stocking feet.

"Dave, we got us a young man with UV conjunctivitis."

I turned to Mrs. Bailey.

"Marcus looked too long at the electrical light of an arc-welding machine. It's so hot it generates ultraviolet light, and that can burn the eyes. Marcus, you're pretty lucky. You could've really gotten hurt. Didn't you see how the man holding the torch wore a big metal mask?"

Dave chimed in.

"Just keep Marcus in a dark room and put cold packs on his eyes. If we're lucky, he should be okay by tomorrow."

Mrs. Bailey pulled a wrinkled, old dollar bill from the upper part of her dress. Before she could hand it to us, we both said "No, thank you."

She laughed and said to Dave, "Now, honey, you don' need me, not frum wha I heard comin' through the walls. She's a screamer, ain't she?"

Dave face turned crimson, and I was thinking, "What the hell is she talking about?"

Then she looked me up and down.

"Betcha I could help ya. Jes' knock on ma door."

She dragged Marcus into the hall by his ear, and as they returned to their apartment, we heard him yell, "But Mama, I didn' mean ta go look theah."

I closed the door.

"What's going on, Country Boy? What did she mean about me stopping by her place?"

"City Boy, for someone who knows everything, you are awfully dumb! She's what my mama used to call a wanton woman."

Then I understood.

"Point taken. Now, what about the 'screamer?'"

His face turned reddened again.

"Uh … well … uh … sometimes Connie stops by when you're on night duty and we … uh…"

"Don't say another word."

Whatever our neighbor was, she was also an angel. She helped save our necks weeks later, when a mob arrived on our doorstep to lynch us. As she so eloquently put it, "Ya'll risked yo' necks ta save Jeremiah. No sense havin' 'em stretched out by a rope. 'Sides, you the wrong color fer lynchin' 'roun' heah."

Mrs. Bailey, I wish you had lived to see the first African American nominated for president.

That night my thoughts once more took me back to my childhood and my neighborhood.

When I was about seven, Papa spent some wonderful times with me. We would walk and walk together. Papa pointed out different shops

and buildings and told me what secrets they held. But some establish-
ments—even as I grew older—Papa never seemed to acknowledge.

"*Che cosa è quello, Papa?*"

What are those, Papa?

He would put his head down and not answer.

As I became a teenager, I stayed out later and later with my friends.
I noticed that, unlike our homes—our little rats' nests of apartments—
some of those mystery buildings would keep their lights on all night.

"Come on, Berto, move those legs."

When I reached seventeen, I became a lord of creation, full of spit
and vinegar. Everybody knew me, and I knew everybody—at least I
thought so. But my friend Sal, as always, surprised me.

In our final year of high school, I had received early acceptance to
university, while Sal had gained early admittance into the mob. We both
felt on top of the world.

Back then I spent most of my free time with my high school friend
Edison, fooling around with electronics. When I would leave his home,
I'd go directly to Dr. Agnelli's clinic. But one weekend, Edison and his
parents were away, and Dr. Agnelli was having some much-needed ren-
ovation done to his examining rooms.

So, as I joked with Sal, I was stuck with him.

Sal rewarded me with a friendly punch to the gut that knocked the
wind out of me. As always, he never intended to hurt me. It's just that
he was just too damned strong.

After the nerve endings in my solar plexus let me breathe again, Sal
helped me up and promised a real treat. He was going to show me
things I had never seen before.

Whenever Sal talked like that, it was usually about something one
didn't talk about with one's mama.

He didn't disappoint me.

"Here ya go, Berto. Yer gonna meet the sweetest girl this side of New York."

Sal was excited, more so than I had seen him in a long time. The last was when he ran to tell me that the beautiful chair he had coveted the day we helped Giuseppe load his wagon had been mysteriously left at his apartment door. I thought he had probably stolen it from the old junk man, but my mind did a one-eighty when I found the small desk, chair, and bookcase I had desired placed on my own stoop.

"Is she in your class at school, big guy?"

He laughed.

"Berto, Crystal is in a class by herself. You'll see."

I noticed we were approaching one of those buildings—the ones Papa never wanted to talk about. But as we crossed the street, Sal suddenly grabbed my arm and steered me into a shop doorway.

"Hey, what gives?"

His grip hurt my arm.

"Look who just got outta that '56 DeSoto!"

It was Sammy Welch and his dad, the defrocked cop. Sam's old man looked proud, as he put his arm on Sammy's shoulder. We could hear the guy's voice loud and clear.

"Now, kid, yer gonna be a man."

Sammy Welch had matured into a tall, fairly decent-looking young man, but he was still his father's son. He let out a nervous laugh as Samuel Welch Sr. steered him inside the apartment with the light in the window.

"Damn, he's gonna see Crystal!"

"Sal, what the hell is going on?"

He turned and grinned at me.

"Geez, Berto, don't you get it?"

He made a motion with his hands, and I turned red. I got it.

We stood in the doorway and waited. It wasn't more than five minutes before a scream shook the walls. We peered out and saw the older Welch dragging his son out of the building. Sammy was trying to button his pants.

"I told you, no rough stuff, least not 'til you're finished! You didn't even make it, did you?"

"Pop, you didn't need to punch her lights out!"

"Don't smart-talk me, you little bastard!"

He struck his son.

"Ow, don't hit me Pa!"

Welch Sr. literally threw Sammy into the car and peeled out from the curb. We waited until it rolled around the corner then, Sal leading the way, ran into the apartment on the first floor, its door wide open.

She sat on a beat-up sofa holding her face. She was one of those women who could be twenty-five or forty. She was tiny, the couch a wide canyon to her petite body, her black hair spotted with blood. I could see bruising around both eyes. When they opened, dark-brown, Levantine irises peered through swollen lids. Her jaw was off kilter, like a child trying hard not to swallow a disliked food. All she had on was a torn and bloodied petticoat.

"Crystal, Crystal, are you okay?"

Sal knelt by her side and tried to pull her hands away from her face. I moved next to him and attempted something Dr. Agnelli had taught me.

"Miss Crystal, let me help you."

She lowered her hands, and Sal and I both gasped, as we saw the blood on her mouth and the jagged, broken ends of her teeth.

"Come on, Sal, she needs help right now."

He cradled her in his arms, lifting her as if she were a feather, and carried her out the door.

I took them to Lyman.

It was Saturday—*Shabbat*—but I knew Lyman Lipschutz would be in his dental office. He lived where he worked. I just didn't know whether he would be willing to see Crystal on his Sabbath.

We climbed the stairs to the second-floor suite, Sal not even breaking a sweat, as he carried the beaten-up and barely conscious woman.

I knocked. No answer. I knocked again, and still no answer.

"Dr. Lipschutz, it's me, Berto Galen. My friend is badly hurt. Please…"

I heard the slow, limping shuffle of the Auschwitz death-camp survivor. The door opened.

"Berto, you know it's *Shabbat*."

Then he saw Sal holding the woman. He saw her face and the ruined teeth and jaw.

"Gott in himmel!"

His own ruined face tried to smile.

"Yes, Berto, I know—German."

He waved us in and guided Sal with his burden to the examining room in back. He pointed to a dental chair, and Sal gently set Crystal down in it. Then he picked up the black, bakelite handset of a phone that had seen its best days and fingered the dial.

Click-whir click, click-whir click, click-whir click.

Seven times that rotary dial spun. I heard the distinctive trill of a number ringing at the other end and then the familiar voice of my mentor.

"Agnelli here. Who's calling?"

"Corrado, it's me, Lyman. Your Berto is here with a young lady. She is in bad shape. Can you help?"

"I'll be right there," the phone voice said, and ended the connection with a click.

Dr. Lipschutz was gently cleaning up the victim's face in preparation for dental X-rays, when the door opened and Dr. Agnelli entered.

"Berto, I'm amazed. You managed to get me to work even when I was closed."

He looked at Sal and glared.

"Did you do this?"

Sal stuttered, "N-n-o, sir. Ask Berto."

As the doctor and dentist examined Crystal, Sal and I took turns describing what we had seen and heard. Both men were muttering imprecations against the Welches, as they assessed the damage.

Except for wincing and uttering an occasional "Ow!" Crystal remained mute. At first I assumed it was because her jaw had been fractured, but as I watched her eyes, I realized that her silence was a response to conflict. Even when Dr. Lipschutz palpated her jaw, she kept her eyes fixed on the wall.

"Young woman, I must do a painful thing now. Your jaw, it is out of joint. I must put it back in place. I will give you something to take the pain away. You will sleep, not feel anything. Hokay?"

Her response surprised us all. Even with an immovable jaw her meaning was clear. She shook her head violently from side to side and made guttural noises close enough to "no!" to be understood.

"Yah, yah, I know. I say same to Nazis. Hokay, hold onto chair."

Dr. Agnelli motioned to me and Sal. We each took places behind the dental chair and held Crystal's hands. Sal put one arm around her chest to steady her.

Dr. Lipschutz gloved his hands.

"Hokay, here we go."

Beads of sweat dotted her forehead. Sal's and mine matched hers, as Dr. Lipschutz stuck both gloved thumbs into her mouth, pushed down, and simultaneously pulled to one side. The intensity of the "snap-click" punctuated Crystal's crescendoing scream. Then she passed out.

"Corrado, quick, hand me the syringe!"

Dr. Agnelli passed the glass tube with its four-inch needle to the dentist who, in turn, quickly injected both sides of Crystal's gums, upper and lower.

Then we all waited.

I forgot to mention: At the sight of the needle Sal passed out. We let him lie there. None of us was strong enough to lift him.

In a few moments Crystal moaned, as she came to. She coughed a few times.

Dr. Agnelli smiled.

"The pain should be gone—at least for now. Our fine dentist is going to see what he can do for your teeth."

He and I stood by, as the little man climbed on his step stool. Again he palpated, examining and making profound "hmms" and "ahhs." He wiggled some teeth. Others he lightly smoothed with a file to remove the rough edges.

"Young lady, you are lucky. I see no major problems. Your teeth not too bad—some gum lacerations. You will be sore coupla weeks."

She tried to thank him, but the numbing medicine made it near impossible. As you know, I had suffered the same experience— and worse—in medical school, when Pat Tilden used me as his guinea pig.

"Corrado, she cannot go back to her apartment. God only knows what might happen."

Dr. Agnelli frowned.

"Lyman, you've got those two spare rooms upstairs, don't you?"

"Yah, yah, good idea. Young lady, you will be my guest, right?"

She shook her head, but Dr. Agnelli turned to us.

"Guys, go back to her place. I'll call Giuseppe. I think his wagon could get her stuff here. Probably not much anyway."

He turned back to Crystal.

"Do you want to press charges against those two bastards?"

She shook her head again, and Sal answered for her.

"No one would believe her or two kids like Berto and me, Doc. You know that."

He was getting angry.

"He is right, Corrado," Dr. Lipschutz interjected. "No one would believe them."

Dr. Agnelli nodded. He gave her a penetrating look.

"What's your real name?"

She sat silent for a moment then mumbled, "Sarah, Sarah Abrams."

The dentist's eyes widened, but he said nothing.

"Do you have any family?"

Another head shake.

"Guys, go fetch Miss Abrams' stuff. Lyman, let me use your telephone."

A short time later we entered the off-limits building again. Crystal's . . . I mean Sarah's apartment door was still open. Sal carefully wrapped her few items of clothing in a clean bedsheet, along with some books and toiletry articles. We took a small table, a couple of lamps, and an ironing board and iron. We left the couch—too many six-legged critters were living in it. Some odd dishes, pots, utensils, and canned goods went into another sheet. There was no icebox to empty.

As we headed outside, I saw that light hanging in the window. I took it down and threw it in the trash.

We waited about ten minutes, before we heard the clip-clop, clip-clop, clip-clop of old Mandy. Sal tossed everything on board, and we swung ourselves up to sit next to Giuseppe.

His bumblebee voice chuckled, "You boys want to ride Mandy?"

We both said no. My rear end still ached from my last ride.

He chuckled once more, as he offered Sal a piece of his chewing tobacco. I thought Sal was going to turn green at the sight.

We unloaded the wagon and climbed the stairs to Dr. Lipschutz's place. He and Dr. Agnelli were sitting in the waiting area.

"Take stuff to third floor, boys. Door has number 3 on it. I left it open."

They headed downstairs.

We hauled the stuff in. It took each of us three trips, and whenever I returned to the wagon, I saw the two men talking with Giuseppe. He was nodding at whatever they were saying.

Then Giuseppe left, and we all returned to the office. We found Sarah up and walking around, looking at the furnishings and shaking her head in disapproval. Even with a mouthful of Novocain she mumbled, "When was the last time you dusted this place?"

Dr. Lipschutz appeared embarrassed, so she muttered, "Oh, never mind."

She was still a bruised lump, but her spirit seemed restored by the attention she had received. Sal moved to put his arm around her, but as he called her "Crystal" she corrected him.

"No, young man, you call me Sarah, Sarah Abrams."

Dr. Lipschutz practically clapped his hands in delight.

Dr. Agnelli also smiled in approval.

"Sarah, we are getting you some furniture for your room upstairs. It will be here soon. On Monday, I will have one of my nurses take you to the clothing store. You will need some new outfits."

She sat down in the dental chair.

"Why?"

"Because..." Dr. Lipschutz said quietly.

We sat there, the older men gently questioning the woman. Where was she from? Why was she there in that building? Did she have any family?

The effect of the numbing medicine was wearing off, and Sarah's voice was becoming more understandable. I sensed that she was feeling the pain but did not want to admit it. I glanced at Dr. Agnelli, and he understood my unspoken question.

Sarah tried answering, but the pain in her jaw was obvious.

"Miss Abrams, I think Dr. Lipschutz has some codeine tablets here. You'd better take one now, before the pain gets worse."

"Yah, yah, I will get the codeine for you, Sarah."

He hurried to his cabinet, unlocked it, and took out a brown bottle. He unscrewed the top, shook out two pills into his hand, and offered them to her.

"Here, take, I will get water."

She accepted the pills from him and waited, while he took a glass from another cabinet. When he saw her staring at it, he held it under running water and rinsed it carefully before filling it. Then he handed it to her.

It suddenly occurred to me that their eyes were fixed on each other, even as she popped the pills in her mouth and took a drink.

I heard Mandy's clip-clop once more and looked out the window. Giuseppe and his wagon were out front, now loaded with bed frame, mattress, dressers, chairs, and more.

"Looks like we got some more stuff to lug," Sal groaned.

We did. I have to admit I was sore after we were done, though it didn't seem to faze Sal.

Soon the five of us surveyed the newly outfitted, third-floor apartment. Giuseppe had even thrown in a Kelvinator refrigerator, the kind with the big coil on top.

Sarah couldn't stop crying, as she went from room to room. While we moved the furnishings, she put on one of the dresses Sal had bundled inside the sheets. She said she wanted to look better for her "four rescuers."

She did—much better.

After we left Sarah and Dr. Lipschutz in the apartment, Dr. Agnelli offered to treat us at the ice-cream parlor down the block. We readily accepted. Two root beer floats apiece later, and Sal and I were belching competitively, while Dr. Agnelli sat sipping the same glass of water. I wondered why he didn't join us in the brain-numbing, ice-cold sugar buzzes. I learned why much later.

Several weeks went by. Out of curiosity I stopped at Dr. Lipschutz's office one day. The first thing I noticed was a new desk in the waiting room with a flower vase on it. The second was Sarah Abrams sitting behind it answering the telephone.

Things were considerably cleaner and brighter.

Just after high-school graduation Sal and I received notes instructing us to go to a particular men's store to be fitted for tuxedos. Picture two Italian boys in monkey suits with yarmulkes on our heads, watching as Sarah Abrams and Lyman Lipschutz stood under the *huppah* before the rabbi, sipping wine from a glass then dropping it on the floor, and Lyman stomping it into a burst of shards, a symbol of the fragility of happiness.

I saw in Lyman's eyes the strength of giants. Sarah's eyes shone with the exorcism of Crystal.

Mazeltov!

The Cat

I visited the cemetery that last day.

Sirius the Dog Star had done its job once again, ushering in August's typical stifling heat and humidity.

And my father had disowned me.

No, I hadn't disgraced the family. I was just going to medical school and—for reasons he wouldn't disclose—Papa wanted me to stay at home instead. Mama remained silent during our first father-son, head-to-head confrontation. She wouldn't tell me why, either.

I carried my two bags down the stairs of the little apartment where I had grown up. I turned back once to see Mama standing in the open doorway then headed out. I still had some final business to do before taking the bus into Newark to catch the train for Richmond.

My legs were good then, trained in the daily campus marathon of running to and from university classes in buildings spread far and wide. They weren't the legs that betray me now with their seven-decades-plus infirmities. Back then they easily carried me, suitcases in hand, past the church-run grammar school I had attended as a child. I followed a familiar path toward the cemetery at the edge of the neighborhood.

I had to say goodbye.

Every year I would visit the graves of my childhood friends and cry.

My conceit would convince me that I cried over the inexplicable loss of young life. The truth that now confronts me is I shed my tears in defense of my ego, the one that assumed I could save people from themselves. But fifty years of dealing with people in their weakest, most demeaning moments has proved the converse: You can only save yourself.

Angie's grave was first on my garden tour. Angelo d'Riggi, dead at age fifteen. He was my first friend. He was there at the beginning, when the dead lady in the river showed me what my life's work would be.

Damn, what a salesman or lawyer he would have been! He was a natural-born con man, the smile never leaving his face, his quick-thinking mind always seeking the angle in every situation.

I stood above the small marker embedded in the ground. I hadn't been able to afford anything larger.

So long, kid.

I walked halfway around that city of the dead and found my second destination. Tomas Pescatore, dead at sixteen. Shy and beanpole thin, Tomas was fast as the wind, the fastest kid in the school.

He just couldn't outrun a bullet.

I wonder if he would have become a track star or maybe an athletic coach.

I hope you're giving the angels a good run for their money, Tommy.

It was hot. I was young then, but even the young feel the effects of late summer, and I found myself wearying. I looked around to see if there were any other visitors, then I found a low-rise headstone to sit on. I was sure its occupant, Mr. Deligianis, wouldn't complain. I placed my two suitcases on the grass then jumped back when something moved.

It hissed at me in annoyance—seven pounds and three shades of brown and yellow, probably a female by its looks and size. I had disturbed its midday nap in the cool shade of the tombstone.

Then I noticed the lop ear on its left side, twisted like a corkscrew. I smiled at the telltale genetic giveaway. It was a descendent of old Patches. What a cat he was!

The female feline regarded me with the total disdain that only a cat can convey then lay down again. I was, as far as it was concerned, dismissed.

Okay, Miss Cat, I'll leave you alone. You're the only one sleeping here who can get up later.

She watched me through half-closed, vertical irises, as I moved away.

I walked farther down the rows and stopped—someone else was there. In roils of wavering heat rising off the ground it seemed to be a young girl dressed in black skirt and white blouse, and wearing a black beret. As I approached, youth left the face, and a familiar voice greeted me.

"Berto? Is that you, Berto?"

Sister Grace Roberta!

Things had changed since I last sat in her sixth-grade class. The long, black, neck-to-ankle gown with white surplice and rectangular wimple serving as a Christian version of a burka—those were gone. Now everything was exposed: the scrawny legs, the surprisingly thin arms and forearms that once wielded a ruler like a whip. Even her face was visible, a large strawberry birthmark on her left forehead naked to the world.

The solar glare continued to blur my vision. The sweat dripped from my forehead and fogged my eyeglasses. But there was something familiar in that face, something I couldn't place. She came forward, the authority figure who had struck fear in the hearts of her peripubertal charges stood before me, the top of her head reaching only my shoulders.

"Sister Grace?"

"No, Berto, no need for deference. I have heard good things about you. Oh, don't look so surprised. I try to follow all my children."

I did look at her with surprise and, yes, a bit of ego gratification at being recognized this many years later.

"So, Berto, what brings you here?"

She was actually smiling! I had never seen Sister Grace Roberta smile. I had seen anger, frustration, disgust, annoyance, and despair on that face, but not happiness. Maybe the old wimple made it impossible to smile.

"Wrapping up loose ends, Sister. I'm leaving today. I start medical school on Monday."

"I heard, Berto. Congratulations! I always knew you'd be a doctor. You were one of the few thinkers I've ever taught."

I blushed. Even in the heat I could feel the rising blood in my face. She was one teacher who could embarrass me with praise. Then she smiled again, and almost instantly her look changed to concern and, maybe, empathy.

"You're visiting your friends, aren't you?"

"Yes, Sister."

Before this delft miniature I was that sixth-grade boy once more.

"You've already said your goodbyes to Angelo and Tomas, haven't you?"

"Yes, Sister."

"Johnny's not here."

I thought of Johnny—Giovanni—and shook my head. I couldn't travel to Pennsylvania, so I had sent flowers every year.

She turned and pointed.

"Salvatore is over there."

"Yes, Sister, I know."

She nodded, gazing at the little monument about ten feet away.

"You put up the markers for them all, didn't you?"

I looked at the ground, at my shoes, as I once had done when she had caught me talking in class. I couldn't look at her. My face burned even more.

"I knew it! You are a romantic! I always had the feeling you and Goethe would have gotten along well, Berto. You were always the brooding Werner in the midst of all those other children. I could understand you being friends with Angelo and Tomas, but why Salvatore?"

I stared past her, and the heat shimmer became an outside theatre screen. I saw my past life unfold before me.

"Berto, wait up."

I had just left the library. I didn't feel up to hanging out with the guys that day. Things were changing within me. My body was in one of those early-adolescent growth spurts, and the awkwardness of my cracking voice, and those first few mountainous zits that would appear overnight to embarrass and torture, were sometimes too much to bear.

"Berto, wait, it's me."

Sal was running full-charge toward me. He had started the downward spiral into adulthood before the rest of us, but he had used those surges of hormones racing through his maturing body to work out and develop his muscles. He towered over my five-foot, one-inch height and was starting to look like King Kong. I think he was the first of our gang to shave.

Sal was upon me before I could step aside, and he swept me up in a bear hug and swung me in the air like a rag doll. I was on some invisible trampoline, as he laughed and easily tossed me above his head one, two, three times and more. Then he put me down.

Thank God we were friends.

"Berto, come on, I'm going to work out. It wouldn't hurt you to try it."

He laughed and poked my nascent flabby gut with a finger that felt like it had pushed through to my spine. As I doubled over from the pain, he caught me and apologized over and over. I had to stop him from crying. He just didn't know his own strength.

Sal's father found out how strong his son had become. His mother had been driven off by what we now call severe spousal abuse—battered spouse syndrome. She had left when Sal was only a year old after serving as a punching bag for her husband's drunken frustrations too long. Neighborhood rumor had it that he had punched her so hard her left eye erupted from its socket. No one knew what had become of her. Some said her husband had killed and buried her. Others said the head injury had made her lose her memory, even the memory of her child.

Sal soon became a surrogate outlet for his father's rages. It was not unusual for him to come to school in those earlier grades with bruises and cuts, the kind produced when someone holds up his arms to protect his face. The thing that remains with me to this day is Sal never cried in school. Even with the bruises, his infectious grin would make the other kids laugh, especially when a ruler-wielding nun was punishing him for some minor infraction.

"Pagliacci?"

Then Sal's hormones kicked in, and the whelp learned to hiss and extend his own claws. Halfway through sixth grade I remember seeing Sal's father stumbling down the street, drunk, with a cast on his left arm and forearm, and multiple bruises on his face. When I asked Sal what had happened, he took on a feral look and laughed. I did not question him further.

As we walked through the neighborhood, on our way to what we euphemistically called the *ristorante* and social club, Sal spotted the big, gray-striped tomcat sitting under the stoop of the building, where the crazy lady lived. The cat was sitting on all fours, slowly pulling apart the body of one of the numerous rats infesting our little luxury community.

"Hey, look! Old Patches is eating out today!"

We both laughed, and the dog-sized head of the big tomcat turned toward us, all the while grinding the rat parts in its jaw. Patches was a neighborhood institution, a feral stray that belonged to no one and everyone in the tenement. He would let you pet him, even stroke his belly. He would roll over and purr loudly and lick your hand. But no one could pick him up. That was the line he drew—except for the Crazy Lady.

On days when the white-haired, gold-star widow who had lost her son in the Great War made her rounds, she pushed her empty baby carriage through the streets. Patches would come out from under the stoop and allow her to pick him up and place him in it. He would sit there on his haunches like royalty, as the woman wheeled his throne, His Majesty turning his head from side to side to accept the encomiums of passersby. His corkscrew ear, which I later learned was genetic and not a war wound from other felines, would serve as antenna to the ambient sounds of the neighborhood. It was said that he had saved the old woman's life on numerous occasions, when she was distracted while crossing a street. His loud tomcat "mowrll" could be heard even by the hearing impaired.

This was a rare moment—I actually saw Sal take on a thoughtful look.

"Berto, that old cat, see . . . he's me. Ain't it the truth? We both gotta make it on our own, don't we? I gotta feeling my job is gonna be ta beat the shit outta rats."

I saw his powerful hands open and close in vise-like clenching.

I lucked out in eighth grade and got a scholarship to Concepción, the local Catholic high school. Angie, Tomas and Sal continued in the local public school, so I didn't see as much of them as before. Freshman year saw Angie getting his throat cut one weekend, when we did have a chance to hang out together.

I couldn't stop the flow of blood. All I could do was hold him, feeling the warmth depart in his agonal death throes.

I heard later that the kid who had done it was found dead with a broken neck.

Sophomore year, Tomas was dating and, as it turned out, the girl was considered the chattel of another guy. The three of us—Tomas, the girl, and I—were walking along the bridge escarpment over the river, when I heard a shot ring out. Almost in slow motion, I seemed to see the front of his head expand and explode forward, as he pitched downward. He was dead before he hit the ground.

Once more I found myself holding a friend's body and rocking back and forth in tears.

Later I heard that the responsible kid was found dead with a broken neck.

High school was a different world, a different culture for me. The kids who went to Concepción were from families living in houses out in the suburbs. They never had awakened and stared into the eyes of a rat crawling across their bed. They never had to sleep in several layers of clothes, because the tenement heating system—right on schedule—failed in the coldest weather.

Still, kids are kids, no matter the social structure or setting, and there are always underdogs. One became my best friend in school, after I found myself unexpectedly taking on Sal's role of tough guy against a school bully.

I told him about that incident once, thinking he'd be proud of me—and he was. But I also saw something else in his face: sadness and maybe a loss of innocence.

Then I didn't see him for quite a while, not until the middle of my senior year at university. It was Good Friday, and I was home on spring break—we called it Easter break then—and I needed to get out of the apartment for awhile. Papa had become more withdrawn. He snapped at the slightest thing I said or did. His initial happiness at hearing of my acceptance to medical school soon had become a sullenness that was uncharacteristic of the man.

I told Mama I was going for a walk—I didn't ask—and she nodded. She knew I was on the verge of manhood, and young males my age were alley cats on the prowl.

I headed down the stairs and took my usual tour of the tenements, even crossing into the forbidden territories of the other ethnics. No one stopped or confronted me. I was still *Dottore* Berto, the one who sewed and patched up anyone who was hurt.

I found myself coming up in front of the *ristorante*/social club, where the Sicilianos and their enforcers would sit, eat, and plan. I saw a familiar face.

"Hey, Berto! Come over, have something to eat."

Sal sat at the front table with an obviously hair-dyed blonde hanging on his shoulder. He had bulked up even more, looking like some Michelin tire man in those pre-steroid days of muscle building.

I was never one to turn down free food.

"*Grazi*, Sal. You're looking stronger than ever."

He turned to the blonde.

"Polly, this is my best friend, Berto. You call him *Dottore* Berto—and only he can call me Sal—*capice*? He's going to medical school soon."

I didn't know how he had found out. Apparently the entire neighborhood knew. He took out a twenty, an unbelievable amount in those days for a young guy to have.

"Here, girl, order what you want. Berto and me we're gonna take a walk and talk."

The girl batted her false eyelashes. I wasn't sure what was real and what wasn't on her.

He got up, put his arm on my shoulder, and steered me out the door. We walked slowly, and he told me how he had been recruited, how he had easily earned the title of enforcer. He wasn't happy.

"Berto, there's got to be something else I can do. I want to do something useful, like what you're going to do."

I looked at the powerfully built man and saw the shadow of the kid's grin behind his sad wistfulness.

"Sal, with your ability, you could become a sports coach in a school."

I laughed and said, "Nobody would act up in your gym classes."

He laughed.

"Me, teach in a school? Maybe I should get a big wooden ruler, too!"

We both laughed some more, as we passed the house where the Crazy Lady lived. Then Sal let out an exclamation.

"Oh, shit, Berto! Look, it's Patches. He don't look too good."

The cat was old now. He had lost a lot of weight. He was lying on his side, taking shallow breaths. He was dying.

We knelt down, and Sal put his hand on the cat. It raised its head slightly, licked his hand, and then died.

Sal ripped off his outer shirt and wrapped the cat's body in it. He stood there in his Stanley Kowalski undershirt in the still-cool April weather.

"Come on, Berto, we owe it to him."

I followed him along the familiar path to the cemetery. We entered the open gate, and Sal knocked on the caretaker's shed. The old man knew us. He stood aside, as my friend grabbed a spade and handed it to me. He beckoned the caretaker to follow us. He did.

Our little procession, a Good Friday burial, ended under a tree near the border of the cemetery. No graves would be dug there. The caretaker looked at the bundle in Sal's arms, held like a beloved baby, and took the shovel from me. He dug the hole deep, and Sal knelt down and placed the cat's body at the bottom. Then the caretaker shoveled the dirt back in. I picked up a large stone lying near the fence and placed it on the fresh mound. Sal crossed himself and stood up.

We walked back to the *ristorante* in silence.

Sal sat down at the same table. The girl had eaten her fill and was letting him know that she didn't appreciate being left alone for so long. I tried to warn her, tried to tell her to shut up. Suddenly my friend's hand shot out and grabbed her neck. It took all my strength to pull that hand away from her.

Sal quieted down. The early spring sun was setting. I noticed that people were leaving, their unfinished plates of food still in place at their tables. The girl stared at Sal, hesitated, and then asked if she could go to the ladies' room. He nodded.

A few minutes passed. The waiter walked over and told Sal that his boss wanted to see him outside. It didn't sound or feel right.

Sal told the waiter to invite the man inside. He said they could share a glass of *vino*.

The waiter laughed nervously.

"Berto, you don't say no to this guy."

He got up, still not showing any signs of being cold in that scanty undershirt, and headed outside. The waiter walked to the back of the eatery.

I could feel what was coming in my bones. I rushed to the door to call out a warning to Sal, when the double blast of a shotgun sent debris through the air. It covered the window, the door, and me.

My hand reached up and felt the warm stickiness of blood. It wasn't mine.

I ran out, as the big car pulled away. Sammy Welch Jr. was laughing in the back window.

Sal was on the sidewalk, a massive hole in his chest, the right side of his head blown away, now matching the red birthmark on his left forehead.

I stood in the cemetery that last day. I really did not have an answer to Sister Grace Roberta's question. In truth the answer needed no words.

I moved toward the little marker set in the ground.

SALVATORE GATTO

The Cat

I looked at the marker in the next plot.

SISTER GRACE ROBERTA

Bride of Christ

Annunciata Moro Gatto

Mother

The Gnomon

He was a giant.

Even back then he was balding, his remaining black hair turning silver-gray along the sides. His nose betrayed his Roman ancestry. He stared down at me above his gold, wire-rim glasses, his sparkling brown eyes observing every nuance. He smiled and turned away from the man sitting on the examining table in the clinic and knelt down to look at me, eye to eye.

"Berto, why are you here?"

He knew who I was—he had delivered me. Mama had been among the countless others who had sought care at his clinic.

How could I tell him? What does an eight year old know? What does an eight year old say to a god?

"Can I watch what you do?"

"Why?"

The words came of their own volition.

"I want to be like you."

He smiled again and nodded then stood up to his full, six-foot height and nodded once more.

And so it began.

I became his shadow, at his side for the next fifteen years until his death.

Dr. Agnelli taught me how to wash my hands with the pungent-smelling, green soap that was ubiquitous in his examining rooms. I followed him from bay to bay, his long, white coat swirling from the speed with which he moved, an ice skater on the worn tile floors. The nurses who worked alongside him, mind readers of his every need, fetched bowls, strange metal instruments, and large glass syringes ending in the dreaded, stainless-steel needles used back then.

I was eight and he was, as I know now, forty-eight. Still I was hard pressed to keep up with him.

He ran what we now call a storefront clinic, and it dealt with all the afflictions that a tenement neighborhood of immigrants of mixed ethnicities experienced. For the most part it was filled with runny-nosed kids like me, women with "women's problems," and the never-ending trauma cases.

I laugh at how primitive it was relative to what I have since learned and practiced, just as my students would laugh, when I used to tell them how I functioned in my own early days as a doctor. But there was a dignity to Dr. Agnelli's practice that the lack of technology made even more precious.

How many doctors today actually touch their patients?

Corrado Agnelli did. He loved all of them and was not afraid to touch them—to deal with the sights and smells and fears exuded by the human organism when something goes amiss. I watched him listen patiently, as he examined a baby boy brought in by a desperate mother who could not lower his fever. His hands, ears, and eyes functioned together, as he observed the flushed skin, the scarlatiniform rash of strep, or the oozing eyes and polka-dot spotting of measles. To him, priest of Aesclepius, the child was a sacred vessel of life, a chalice to be handled reverently.

If it was one of those rare, fortunate cases where a baby was well, the best medicine he could offer was sympathetic reassurance. He would laugh, as the infant rewarded his efforts by showering him with urine or spitting up curdled milk on his hands.

The old, those lucky or unlucky enough to have reached an age of increasing infirmity—the downward spiral of the life cycle looming over them—presented their numerous complaints: shortness of breath, chest pains, rheumatism. Such conditions actually appeared far less frequently than today, because most of the tenement population met the Bone Man before these degenerative conditions had time to take hold. Malnutrition, physical and emotional abuse, even the stress of repeated childbirth, all served the whim of the dark angel.

What appealed most to my young boy's mind were the blood-and-guts trauma cases, the product of the ethnic clashes in the neighborhood. They unsettled and saddened the normally unflappable doctor the most.

"Berto, come here. Our young man, Lianto, see what he has brought upon himself?"

I looked at the teenage boy sitting there holding a forearm filleted by another teen's homemade knife. The skin lay split open, thin layers of fat and underlying muscle exposed by the sharp edge of uncontrolled rage.

"Watch, Berto. Lianto, move your fingers."

The boy's limb became a puppet on a stick. As his fingers moved, I could see the bunching and relaxing of the brown-red muscles encapsulated in pearly sheaths, their long, yellow-white tendons the strings of a violin in motion.

"Ah, good. Berto, we've just tested Lianto's nerves and tendons to see if any were cut. Since he can do those movements, they weren't. Now let's put this young man back together."

He poured bowl after bowl of irrigating-cleansing solution into the wound. As he told me later, it was the most important step: Never close a dirty wound.

I saw him take a syringe from the tray held by his acolyte nurse. The young man's eyes dilated at the sight of the needle, but Agnelli shushed him.

"Lianto, this will hurt a helluva lot less than the knife that sliced you. And once it's in, you won't feel any pain. Now take a big breath and hold it."

Like magic he inserted the needle and removed it from under the edges of skin, each time leaving raised areas where he had deposited the pain-relieving, anesthetic liquid. Finally the plunger reached the bottom of the glass barrel.

"Lianto, we're going to let you sit a moment, while the medicine does its job. Then we'll close you up."

He motioned for me to follow, and we walked away from the cot where the boy lay.

"Learn from this, Berto. This should never have happened. Live your life, but never lose control."

Would that I had heeded such advice.

We returned to the patient, and the *dottore* slipped on rubber gloves. The nurse, wraith-like, appeared once more with a covered tray. When she removed the lid, I saw the magic tools: the needle holder, the forceps, the silk thread, and several sizes of curved needles.

Agnelli threaded a needle and grasped it with the holder then turned to me.

"It is important that we bring the skin edges together just right."

Then he recited a mantra that has stayed with me for nearly seven decades: "Equal edges come together in prayer."

Another old-man's memory flashback: In Corrado Agnelli's day, they packed silk suture thread inside glass capsules filled with sterile water. The filaments had to be carefully broken open and removed then threaded onto individual needles. By the middle of my own career, metal staples and skin glue that set almost instantly took the place of prepackaged needles and nylon or other synthetic thread combinations.

The march of progress!

My tenth birthday was memorable. Papa surprised me with a brass belt buckle he had made from scraps at the foundry. He had brazed my name onto it. He attached it to my belt, and I could not stop touching it and looking at it. Even now I go to my dresser drawer and pull it out, the leather strap long rotted and gone. I rub my fingers over the raised letters: BERTO.

It is not unusual for that remnant of my youth to become wet with tears, as I remember what happened later on my birthday.

The brawls on Hamilton Street were worse than usual that year. My friends Angie and Tomas were, like me, typical ten year olds, and we could not resist going to watch the fights. That is where I received my true baptism—I experienced what it means to be responsible for another person's life, when I used makeshift tools to stop the mortal bleeding of one of the brawlers.

It also taught me how fast news travels on the neighborhood jungle telegraph.

"Berto, you did a foolish thing!"

I had gone to the clinic after school. Dr. Agnelli had been busy delivering the baby of one of the neighborhood women. It was the one procedure he would not let me observe.

He walked out of the makeshift delivery room, the same one where my mother had given birth to me—where he had delivered me. His gown was covered in blood, amniotic fluid, and other stains I didn't recognize. I could hear the cry of the newborn infant coming from behind the curtain, and I saw the anxious father, still dressed in his foundry work clothes, being admitted to see his wife and new daughter. I wondered if that was how my father looked and behaved when I had entered the world.

My mother never failed to remind me that I would not have existed but for the skills and persistence of the *dottore*. He had guided her and Papa through the loss of four other pregnancies. And when I began to form within her, Mama immediately sought his counsel.

She would smile, and Papa would nod, as she quoted—word for word—Dr. Agnelli's visit, where he confirmed her pregnancy then reassured her that this time she would deliver a healthy baby.

He tossed the soiled gown into a cloth bag, removed his gloves, and threw them into another container. Then he sat down. Deliveries were one of the few activities that truly exhausted him. When I asked him why, his remark seemed cryptic to my young mind.

"Deliveries bring the triple responsibility of mother, child, and father. Harm one and, like dominoes, they all collapse."

Dear God, how I remember witnessing my first delivery death as a student, and how those words came back to haunt me.

He looked at me.

"Berto, why did you put that young man at risk?"

I shook my head, confused by his words. He was bleeding to death, and I had sewed up the wound and stopped the bleeding. What had I done wrong? Then I started to tremble and felt hard pressed to keep from crying.

Dr. Agnelli put his hand on mine.

"No, don't cry, Berto. I guess I have mixed feelings about what you did. I'm proud of your initiative, your willingness to help. But there are many things you do not yet know about the human body. Maybe next time, God forbid that there be one, the safest thing you could do would be to put pressure on the wound to keep blood loss from killing your patient. Your friends could then run and get help."

He knew there was a big unspoken "if" in his advice. The inhabitants of my neighborhood would sooner die than call the police or go to a hospital.

I remained quiet, and I think he knew I would not heed this particular advice. There were so many more fights, so many wounds. So from that time on he strove to teach me the hidden messages, the warning signs to watch for. In his own way he kept me from committing errors of omission that would kill just as quickly as a knife or bullet.

"Berto, come, wash and gown up."

I was not quite fifteen. He no longer had to squat to look at me eye to eye, because I was almost as tall as he was. And I could easily follow him around. But this was the first time he had asked me to put on the sacerdotal gown, cap, and gloves.

"Berto, you are old enough to understand and appreciate the miracle of new life. Mrs. Recalde's contractions are now at the point where she is ready to deliver. Do you want to assist?"

It took the loud and repeated warnings from the nurse to keep me from rushing through the essential hand-and-forearm scrub, the aroma of the green soap by then a familiar perfume to my nose. My nerves tingled, my heart rate uncountable, and I realized why he had been showing me his textbooks on obstetrics for the past two months.

That day I helped in the birth of my schoolmate Pepe's little brother.

As the expression goes, there are some things most people should not know, one of which is the ingredients in sausage, and the other the process of childbirth. I suctioned the mucus from the beet-red, squalling baby boy's mouth then watched the nurse apply the clamp to the cord. Dr. Agnelli handed me the placental lifeline and showed me how to count the number of blood vessels inside its umbilical cord.

Another indelible memory: Mrs. Recalde, exhausted but smiling, took her new baby in her arms and looked up, saying *"Gracias, Dottore Agnelli. Gracias, Dottore Berto."*

When I reached the age of self-awareness, that difference in brain chemistry when perception of self versus others occurs—the beginning of adult socialization and trying to understand the motivations of others—I sought to understand Corrado Agnelli.

"Dottore, do you have any children?"

His face darkened, the creases on his forehead an inverted V.

"Berto, are you sure you want to know about me?"

I suddenly felt stupid, and my face must have shown my lack of understanding.

He looked at me, his head almost bald except for the monk's tonsure of hair around the edges. It was an unusually quiet time, the waiting area clear of the ailing. He pulled up two chairs, straddled one backwards, folded his arms across the chair back and pointed to the other. I sat.

"Berto, I have dreaded this moment. I knew it would come, but I hoped it wouldn't."

I felt even more stupid.

He laughed at my facial expression then rested his head on his folded arms.

"I see the direction your life is headed, Berto. You remind me so much of myself back in Rome, following the famous *dottores'* coattails and asking questions.

"My father was an *avvocato,* a lawyer, and my parents had always assumed I would become one, too. He had high hopes I would also go into politics. He would tell us stories of how he had been invited to lunch with King Victor Emmanuel and all the notable people of the Eternal City.

"My uncle was also a politician and, to my good fortune, a wiser man than my papa. Like your grandpapa Pasquale—yes, your father has told me the story many times—my Zio Marcello also heard the rising drumbeat of war. He was a wealthy man. He paid for my transport to the United States and set me up in boarding school then university.

"By the time I graduated from Columbia I had found a wife among the nursing staff. She had great plans for me."

He stopped and stared into some distant past, his eyes filming with tears. He wiped his face on the sleeve of his white coat.

"Sorry, Berto, see what happens when you get to be an old man?"

He smiled at me, and I found myself staring into the soul of the man I idolized.

Yes, Corrado, I am much older than you were then and I do understand—now.

He took a breath and continued.

"I told my wife I wanted to run a clinic for the poor. She knew I came from a wealthy family back home, but I had never told her of the beggars, the destitute who lined the back streets of Rome, and the priests in their finery who ignored them as they walked past. I swore that I would return God's gift by working among the poor.

"And then I received word. My father had passed away and, shortly afterwards, so did my Zio Marcus. They left everything to me.

"It was a strange confluence of events. My wife Lizabetta had just given birth to our son Marcellus. She made it known that she expected me to open a practice in an affluent section of New York. Over and over she reminded me that our son would not grow up in squalor. And then those two damned telegrams and the Special Delivery letter arrived from the lawyers managing my father's and uncle's estates.

"Berto, you can't even imagine the amount of money. It was so much that, had I so wished, I could have quit work forever!

"My wife saw the papers, and her eyes glowed."

Dr. Agnelli stared at the worn tile floor of his clinic, seeing God only knows what past images in their reflections. His shoulders trembled slightly, and it shocked me to realize that the man I worshipped as a deity really was a man.

He looked at me, his eyes once again moist.

"Berto, she left me. My wife took my son and left me, when she understood that my life was here. She called this place my 'other woman.'

"I haven't seen my son in fifteen years."

Then I saw something else in his eyes: pity.

"Yes, Berto, I see in you a reflection of my own life. Don't make the same mistakes I did."

It was the first and last time we talked about such things.

I continued to walk in his shadow on the days I had to spare while traversing the pitfalls of high school and college.

Then it was my final day at home. I was leaving, against my father's wishes, for medical school.

Those painful last words, *"Non ho figlio"*—I have no son—still rang in my ears, and I sought solace with my mentor.

Dr. Agnelli looked tired. He was sixty-two, and the life he led, the daily giving of all that he had, was taking its toll. His eyes drooped from fatigue, his spirit no longer quite ready to meet the next challenge. I noticed the fine tremor in his hands and the slight uncertainty in his gait. He grimaced, as he sat down in the time-worn desk chair and rubbed his fingers. There was a faint aroma to his breath, as if he had been chewing gum.

I let out my feelings and, as I had hoped, he reaffirmed my dream of becoming a doctor and told me never to give up that dream. Then he bore into me with those penetrating, perceptive eyes.

"You see it, don't you, Berto?"

"Yes, *Dottore*. Are you taking insulin for your diabetes?"

"What else, Berto?"

"You have early Parkinsonism and arthritis."

"Bravo, boy," he replied, his hands moving awkwardly in a clapping motion.

He smiled at me once more.

"Berto, I am going to work as long as I can. I had hoped to be able to turn this over to you one day…"

Pausing, he already knew the answer but asked the question anyway.

"*Dottore* Berto, do you think I can make it until you finish school?"

I stared at the floor.

He stood up and extended his hand to shake mine. Then he hugged me and, before I could react, he had slipped ten twenty-dollar bills into my shirt pocket.

As I turned to leave, my eyes blurred, I heard him say, *"Buona fortuna, Dottore* Berto."

Twice during my freshman year at medical school I received telegrams announcing the passing of my papa and mama. I learned to hate those paper messengers of the dark angel, as had Corrado.

I received a third one just as I finished that year. It was from one of his former nurses. Dr Agnelli wanted to see me.

He was missing one leg.

Diabetes had taken its toll, and the surgeon's knife had removed the gangrenous limb. It didn't help.

He was sixty-three then, much younger than I am now. He was alone, and he was dying. I was the only one there by his bedside. His wife and son had not returned.

"The price I paid for the life I led," he half-whispered.

He turned his face away and cried quietly, a living cautionary tale for my own chosen path. Then he turned back to face me and asked, point-blank, "Do you really want to be like me?"

I held the hand of the man who had been like a second father.

He smiled wanly, and I could barely make out his words.

"I knew you would come, Berto."

I was beginning my sophomore year, when a large manila envelope and a shipping box arrived at the Church Hill apartment in Richmond that I shared with my roommate, Dave. He sat with me, as I opened the letter from a prestigious law firm in Manhattan.

Corrado Agnelli had named me his heir and trustee of the money left him by his father and uncle. We gasped at the eight-figure sum written on the bank statement. At last I understood how he had funded his free clinic for decades.

I opened the box. His death certificate lay on top, and under it his birth certificate. Under that, several albums of aged photos carried me back to pre-World War I Rome and the happy young boy staring intently at the camera. School and university diplomas testified to the superior abilities Corrado Agnelli had demonstrated.

Under more official documents and awards lay a faded, yellow newspaper clipping. It contained an article about a woman and her fifteen-year-old son found murdered in a crime spree through an exclusive New York neighborhood.

I called the attorney listed on the letterhead. I instructed him to contact Corrado's alma mater and offer to establish the Agnelli Chair in Community Medicine. I specified that the school would be obligated to use the income from the trust fund to run free neighborhood clinics, Agnelli Clinics, staffed by interns and residents.

Then I sat back and cried.

There is a little church cemetery on the outskirts of Newark, New Jersey. Despite the surrounding neighborhood decay, it is preserved and kept in spotless condition—another proviso of the trust fund.

There is a special gravestone in that cemetery. It is six feet tall and casts a large and moving shadow as the sun traverses the heavens.

It is what Corrado Agnelli was to me—a Gnomon.

Has my own life cast even half the shadow, half the goodness and influence, of this good and humble man?

The Tree

We moved in on that firecracker-hot Fourth of July.

We sat under the backyard maple, Cathy and I. It was our first house, our first home together.

The tree was there when we bought the place. Like the two of us, it wasn't young, but it wasn't old either.

It took truckloads of dirt to fill in and level off the never-before-cared-for yard. Remnants of decade-old construction debris lay scattered, sometimes erupting like deformed teeth from the dense, clay soil that allowed water to sit in dirty mud-lakes after a heavy rain.

Somehow, despite its environs, that maple tree had managed to sprout and grow, ignoring the ongoing commotion while the house was being built.

By now I had become a (young) middle-ager, still full of energy and strength—and hope. I had lost my first wife, Leni, while I was in my twenties. Now Cathy had entered my middle ground to fill the void. I was strong then, strong enough to place the concrete benches I had purchased from the local stone mason around the tree's base at Cathy's direction.

I had completed the circle.

In the summer the maple's thousands of five-pointed leaves shaded us from the fierce Northern Virginia heat, amplifying even the slightest breeze into cooling air currents. And, like every love relationship, the tree and I had our off moments. A city kid like me did not appreciate its early spring dusting of pollen on my car windshield or the uncountable, whirligig seeds that coated the parking lot. In the fall, it did its best to give me aerobic exercise by casting a thick carpet of leaves to rake, as the chilly gusts presaged the cold winter to come.

Truth be told, I was annoyed that first autumn, venting my spleen at nature's intrinsic messiness.

Berto the boy never had to rake leaves.

Cathy must have seen my frustration, because she walked out, put her arms around me, and reminded me how hard our tree had worked to give us shade during the summer heat.

Her kisses always defused my ire.

"Besides," she said as she patted my tummy, "you really do need the exercise."

So I chased her around the leaf pile, until she let me catch her, and we both fell into it and laughed our heads off. Who says romance belongs only to the young?

That night, as we lay in bed, we talked about our tree. She was amazed that I grew up in a place devoid of such wonderment. I laughed and tried to make light of the tenacious, noxious weeds that grew through the cracks in the ancient sidewalk stones and substandard concrete that sporadically dotted my childhood territory.

"Well, Cathy, those weeds were green—sometimes—and they were survivors."

"My God, Tony, did you hear what you just said?"

For her, as it was with my beloved Leni, I would always be Tony. I raised an eyebrow and whispered, "Who's this Tony? I'm Berto."

She giggled, and I tickled her toes with mine.

"Berto is a kid's nickname, and from what I've seen, you ain't no kid no mo'!"

She turned toward me, her eyes wide.

"You really don't see it, do you?"

I do a good imitation of stupid—so good it's hard to tell the real from the acting.

Sometimes even I wasn't sure. I opened my mouth but she placed a finger over it and said, "No, Tony, don't deny it. In your own way you just described yourself!"

My wonderful Cathy began to cry.

Why do women do that?

No amount of levity, no gross comparisons of forest animals with tenement rats, cockroaches, and flies, could sway her.

What could I do? A husband does not ignore a crying wife. I kissed her and held her, as we fell asleep.

I tried to dream that night. I sought respite and insight in my childhood, but this time Berto's world eluded me.

Why?

The question was the eight-hundred-pound gorilla sitting at the edge of my consciousness, as I went through my routine of patient care the next day. As lunchtime approached, I asked my secretary, Virginia, to give me ten uninterrupted minutes, while I stepped outside.

I walked down the asphalt pathway toward the backyard parking lot and stopped in front of the maple. Most of its leaves were down now, and I was glad that I had worn my pullover sweater. The late-fall breezes were brisk, moving the bare limbs like some invisible conductor at a spirit concert.

Four sturdy, major branches extended upward for about ten feet above the main trunk in a voiceless hallelujah. The tree was stocky, like me, not tall but not short, its base over two feet in diameter.

I moved toward the trunk and ran my hand over its corrugated bark.

I patted it and whispered, "I'm sorry I yelled at you yesterday."

I turned back up the walk, looking at the final remnants of flower husks in the patch of garden I had cultivated as a memorial to Leni. I bent over and picked up one of the maple whirligigs that had lain there all summer and placed it in my pocket.

Nothing stays the same. The universe continues its inexorable march toward entropy, sometimes slow, sometimes inexplicably fast. Despite my best efforts the years passed, and with each change of season I would faithfully rake up the leaves from the tree that brought Cathy and me respite during those hot summer days and evenings.

That particular fall was a gentle one but still chilly enough to prompt the neighbors to light up their fireplaces. I had finished collecting the leaves and carefully placing them in the mulch bin to compost for next year's garden. I went back to give my ritual tree trunk pat, when I saw the loosened bark on one large limb. Something was wrong.

The next day the arborist shook his head and told me he needed to remove the limb. He described it as something akin to cancer and said removal was the only way to save our tree.

Cathy and I watched, as the man excised the twelve-inch-diameter branch and carted it away.

She cried, and so did I.

The following spring Cathy walked in after a visit to the garden.

"Tony, I think another limb needs to come off."

The remaining two limbs did yeoman work that summer and seemed even more filled out than usual. We did not lack for shade.

Three more years passed and, foolish human that I am, I assumed that our lives had achieved some balance, some homeostasis, where nothing changed except the hours of the day and the days of the week. And then I heard Cathy's words that quiet dinner time.

"Tony, I don't feel well."

Technology confirmed my worst fears. My mind fixed on one thought: If Cathy had only been a tree, then the part of her inhabited by the malignant crab could have been removed as easily as a maple's limb.

Three months later, I sat under our tree after Cathy's funeral. It was raining, but the remaining two limbs provided an umbrella against nature's tears ... but not my own.

I entered the slippery slope of old age alone. Now my memorial garden served to remind me of Leni and Cathy, and the maple tree continued its yearly cycle of death and resurrection ... and I understood.

Then the rain intensified. It grew monsoon-like and persistent—strange for our locale. By then the maple was in full leaf, and for several days it bravely withstood the wind gusts and sheets of water. Safely inside I stared out the back window and wondered whether it was time for me to build an ark.

That evening I sat listening to Moussorgsky's "Night on Bald Mountain." The pelting rain kept time against the windows.

And then I heard a muffled "whumpf."

Sometimes on the battlefield that's all you hear before the explosion sends its lethal burst of shell fragments to carry your friends to Valhalla.

I ran out the back door, ignoring the drenching downpour. The outside house light illuminated the carnage.

I moved toward the maple, now lying across the lawn, its branches still quivering. I held them until they stopped moving. And then I sat down beside it until dawn.

I could not watch as the arborist removed it the next day.

The rain had stopped. After the workmen had gone I put on my pullover sweater and walked outside in the early evening. There was a void where my friend had been. I reached into my pocket to warm my hand against the damp chill.

I felt something.

I pulled it out.

It was that little maple seed.

I planted it.

R.A. Comunale is a semi-retired physician in family practice and specialist in aviation medicine who lives and works out of his home office in McLean, Virginia. He enjoys writing, gardening, electronics, pounding on a piano, and yelling at his dimwitted cat. He describes himself as an eccentric and iconoclast.

The cat is seeking legal counsel.